THE
WITCH'S
COMPLEMENT

Bite of Magic – Book 1

LUCILLE YATES

The Witch's Complement

Book and Cover design by Maria Spada
Edits by Black Lotus Editing
Book Formatting Templete by Derek Murphy @Creativindie

First Edition: May 2021

ISBN: 9781736969717

Kitty Hex Press

www.lucilleyateswrites.com

DEDICATION

To my husband and son.
To my mom and my sister.
Thank you for always believing in me and supporting my
dreams.

CHAPTER 1

The bells on the door clattered as it swung open. Jesi pushed inside, closing it behind her. She leaned her back against the door, her eyes closed. The scent of sage and lavender filled her nose, overpowering the other aromas. She inhaled it slowly. The pounding of her heart faded from her ears. Her breathing slowed. She pushed herself off the door, straightened her blazer, and pulled her bag back onto her shoulder. She inhaled once more and opened her eyes.

The store before her was as it always was. Display racks stood on the hardwood floors filled with bags of assorted teas, herbs and spices, gifts, and jewelry. Shelves lined the partial brick walls filled with rocks, crystals, and books. All organized by Maggie, her cousin and the owner, who was shooting quick glances at Jesi from behind the counter.

Jesi gave her a tight smile and began walking toward her. Maggie held her own forced grin as she spoke with the customer she was helping. Maggie's light purple choppy bob blended in with the brightly decorated store. She drummed her fingers on the counter that had books stacked high above her head.

"Thank you so much, Hayley," Maggie said. "I'll be sure to remember that when Roger makes his next order."

They smiled at each other, and Hayley turned to walk toward the door. As she passed Jesi, she gave a fake smile. Jesi veered away from Hayley right before she bumped shoulders with her. She rolled her eyes as the door closed behind her.

"She used to be so nice," Maggie said as Hayley left the store.

"I remember," Jesi said. "What happened?"

"I don't know, but Roger spends enough money for me to ignore her. Want some tea?"

"No. Just a chair," Jesi said, taking a seat behind the counter. "Anyone else here?" She glanced around the empty shop. Her eyes lingered on the door labeled 'The Magic Room'. Anyone not familiar with the supernatural read the sign as 'Employees Only'. Being part of a long line of witches, Jesi saw through the glamor.

"No. Only Hayley and her new tattoo so far today," Maggie said.

"That's why she looked extra smug."

"Yes. Roger did it himself. 'It's runic for Gift. Roger says I'm a gift to the world. But you wouldn't know much about runes'." Maggie's impression of Hayley was spot on. "Looks like a bunch of crisscrossed lines if you ask me.

Anyway, what happened?"

"I don't know what you're talking about," Jesi said. She wasn't sure she wanted to share her morning with anyone. She wanted to digest it all first.

"Really?" Maggie said. "You barge in here, slam the door, practically sling the bells across the room, and end up panting against the door. But you don't know what I'm talking about." Maggie looked back at the door. "Were you chased? Did Mr. Fuller's dog get off his leash again? I know Bunny looks fierce, but his name is Bunny and he just wants to lick you."

"No," Jesi said. She leaned back into the chair and looked at the ceiling. How could she explain this to Maggie? Or anyone else, for that matter?

"Then something happened at the police station? What did you find out?"

"Not much." Jesi put her head in her hands. "It's so embarrassing."

"Really?" Maggie dragged out the word. Her southern accent came through. She leaned forward and rested her head on her hands. "Start from the beginning." Jesi stared at Maggie. She knew she had to tell her. But did Maggie have to look so eager?

"You can tell me or you can tell Aunt Sylvia," Maggie added. Aunt Sylvia was the coven leader. Jesi never wanted to tell Sylvia about her fiasco at the police station.

"Fine. I'll tell you." Jesi crossed her arms over her chest. "So, I walked into the precinct. I have my suit on that surprisingly still fits after sitting in my closet for a year, I have my bag, my business cards, and a plan. I walk up to the desk and request to speak to the detective in charge of Aiden Jacob and Pattie Nelson's disappearances. After explaining that I was the families' attorney, they pointed me towards two desks on the right side of the room."

"Okay, I'm going to stop you right here and say your suit is on point. Go ahead."

"Thank you. I go to the desk. There I met a Detective Thompson—tall, dark, and pervy. He kept looking me up and down. From Thompson, I learned that they know little about the case. We actually have more information than the cops right now. Also, he isn't really working on it. Detective Chuck Massey is the lead on the case, but his assigned partner just had a baby, so Thompson is filling in when needed. Then, Detective Massey shows up while I'm trying to get Thompson to stop shaking my hand. Massey is tall, blond, blue eyes, and has way too much confidence. Typical detective."

"I like him already. Go on."

"You would. First, I ask if he has any updates. He says no. I explain that my clients want to be in the loop. He pushes back on sharing information and we banter back and forth. I hand him my card, which he doesn't look at, and I shake his hand. And I find out nothing."

"That's it? How is that embarrassing?"

"No. I saw *nothing*. No vision, no past, no present. There was no gleaning. When I shook Thompson's hand, I saw his entire life story. His mom, sisters, the partner he actually works with, how he likes his coffee. I shook Massey's hand and zilch. For the first time in a year, I touch someone and don't see anything." Jesi rubbed her face with her hands. She only got the power to glean a year ago. She saw the past of anyone she touched. Even the briefest of nudges filled her head with a person's history. If her skin touched another's skin, she could write their biography. What if she was broken? Hope filled her for just a moment. She could get her life back.

"Wow. I don't know what to say. Do you think he's a witch, too? But how is that embarrassing?" Maggie's eyebrows bunched together.

"I kinda didn't let his hand go. I actually grabbed on with my other hand. I kept looking from our hands to his face. Back and forth. Back and forth."

"No," Maggie whispered.

"Yes," Jesi said. "I was so flustered. He actually pulled away. My brain kicked in and I let go. I thanked him for his time and I ran out of there. I raced here. What's going on?"

Maggie was looking at Jesi with wide eyes and an open mouth. "Well, there are several, uh, reasons this could happen," she said breaking the silence.

"Like what?" Jesi asked. "You said witch, but I was thinking demon. Or maybe I'm hopeless as a witch and should retire early, then go back to my regularly scheduled life."

"Unlikely," Maggie said. "He could be a witch that has a charm to reject other's magic. What did he smell like? When you touched him, did you feel anything at all?"

"Well, he smells amazing. Like cedar and spring rain.

And when we touched, there was a little static and a feeling of warmth moved up my arm."

"Cedar and spring rain? Did you hug him?"

Jesi shook her head.

Maggie continued, "Tell me about the static. Was it a lot of static? Anything else you noticed in that moment?"

"Normal static, but instead of making me jerk my hand back, I just latched on and I couldn't look away from his eyes."

"He could be a demon. You said his eyes were blue. Did they flicker while you were holding his hand?"

"No. I'm sure. There was something about him I couldn't tear my eyes away from."

"Well, there is a thing, but I want to look into it first."

"Out with it," Jesi said, pointing at Maggie.

"I don't want to give you the wrong idea, in case I'm wrong," Maggie said, drumming her fingers on the counter.

Jesi stared at Maggie. "Out with it," she said again. Maggie had an annoying habit of never being wrong, yet she always second guessed herself. She was a bit of a research queen. Normally, Jesi appreciated her thoroughness, but right now, she needed answers.

"He could be your complement," Maggie said with a small shrug.

"What's a complement?" Jesi asked.

Maggie's drumming stopped. "Really?" She stood up and went into the room behind the counter. Maggie had a workshop there where she put together teas, potions, and spell bags.

Jesi didn't move. She was overwhelmed. She was sinking. Law school fooled her into thinking she would never feel overwhelmed again. Even at her first job as a lawyer at the local law firm, Goldstein, Moore, and Smith, she never buckled under the load. Being the lead on a case for the first time was empowering, not overwhelming. Then a year ago, Jesi's great-grandmother, Gigi, passed away.

Gigi was a force all her own. She was the leader of the Moonlight Oak Coven. She had respect and knowledge and opened this shop decades ago. Most importantly, Gigi had the witch power to glean. Many viewed this as a dangerous power, to know everything about a person with a single touch. Invasive powers, like gleaning, were only gifted to one witch at a time, or so the old books said. Once that witch dies, it moves on to another one, usually one within a different coven. Often a different country. When Gigi died, the ability to glean, much to everyone's surprise, went to Jesi.

As a kid, Jesi was happy she didn't get a witch power. She and Maggie were the first children in three generations to not develop one. She stopped paying attention to all the coven lessons, not that she had paid much attention before. She grew up and pursued a career. Then Gigi died. When Jesi woke up that day, everything felt energized. Her hair cooperated; all the lights were green on the way to work. She got a good parking spot. She felt vibrant. Then she shook a colleague's hand and everything stood still. She dropped to the floor, flooded with images of his past, good and bad. She couldn't breathe as everyone started touching her, trying to help her up. Asking what was wrong. That was the day overwhelming took on a new meaning. Jesi ran to her office and barricaded the door. She called the first person who came to mind – Gigi. But Gigi didn't answer. Maggie did and came to her rescue. She brought her gloves and a hat, 'just in case'. Maggie was the one who deserved this gift. Jesi thought it was a curse.

Today, she thought gleaning would become that gift everyone told her it was. She could help find the missing children and she failed. It failed. And here she sat, disappointed in herself and delighted at the same time. She felt like the worst sort of person.

Maggie came out of the back room with a stack of books in her arms.

"I didn't know there were books in there," Jesi said.

"There aren't." Maggie put the books on the counter. "They're from the library connected to it."

"I always forget about that room," Jesi muttered, grabbing the book off the top. Old Magik and Companions by Joseph Starland.

"And where are the books you took home last night?" asked Maggie.

"In the car," Jesi said. She turned the page and skimmed. "All I found was a good collard greens recipe."

"Okay," said Maggie, "so, a complement is a person perfectly suited for an active witch, one with a witch power. It's like a familiar that's humanoid," Maggie said as she flipped through the next book on the stack.

"How come I've never heard about this?" Jesi asked.

"Well, for one, you didn't pay attention to the lessons," Maggie said. "And not many witches find their complement. The only pair I know about were Gigi and Gramps. Oh, here is one description. 'If a witch is pure and has the luck of old, she may come across her complement. She will know her complement when her innate power has no effect on the chosen. Complements will become the witch's closest confidant and, in most cases, her spiritual and physical partner'."

"'Spiritual and physical partner'?" Jesi said. "What am I supposed to do? Marry him? What does spiritual partner mean? This is insane."

"Calm down, girl. This book was written in 1200 and translated several times," Maggie said.

"Does that mean none of the spells I cast will work on him?" she asked.

"No," Maggie said. "Your innate ability won't work, so no gleaning. You can do anything else to him... That came out wrong. Besides, we have more books to reference."

"Well, I don't want to reference them," Jesi said. "We have more important things to do. Aiden and Pattie are still missing and we don't know where they are."

"Yes. And if a cop is your complement, we might get the upper hand," Maggie pointed out. "We need all the help we can get."

"What does that mean?" Jesi crossed her arms. Was she expected to charm a cop for his help? Did Maggie want her to put out for the upper hand?

"It means that getting to know this detective could help us find the kids. So, it wouldn't hurt you to learn more about him." Maggie pulled another book and began skimming.

"That's the weakest argument you've ever given me," Jesi said.

"What can I say?" Maggie shrugged. "I'm tired and not getting enough sleep. I've been scrying, reading, and calling in favors for the last two days."

"Like I said. More important things to do, like pretending you can see into the future," Jesi smirked. "So, why do you want to look into complements?"

"Fine, the psychics are scrying. And my brain needs something it can solve." Maggie looked up, smiling. "So, is he cute?"

"Is he cute?" Jesi said. "That's what you want to know?"

"Yeah. Let me live vicariously through you for a bit."

"You don't need to live through me. You're younger than I am. Go get your own hottie."

"Hottie? So, he's a hottie?" Maggie asked. She wagged her eyebrows and propped her elbows on the counter with her head in her hands. "You mentioned he is tall, blonde, blue eyes, and oozes confidence."

"Never say 'oozes confidence' again." Jesi pretended to retch.

"But he's confident. I bet he has great posture. Did he give a half smile when he shook your hand?"

Jesi raised an eyebrow. "Who are you thinking of right now?"

"Detective Chuck played by a young Daniel Craig."

"I don't need this kind of stress. And what happens if I tell him about all this? He becomes an exposure risk." Jesi rubbed her temples, then moved to her face. She should have kept her mouth shut.

"I'm trying to de-stress the situation. Ten minutes of daydreaming will do us some good. Besides, there is a spell that can erase his knowledge of the supernatural." Maggie shrugged. Jesi squinted at her. How many people has she used that spell on?

"Fine, moving forward. Say this guy is my complement and not an evil witch demon guy, what should I be expecting?"

Maggie looked at Jesi with a blank expression. She then gestured toward the books. "Have books. Will read," Maggie said. "We could always talk to Aunt Sylvia."

"No," Jesi said. "Not yet. I don't want her involved until I have a handle on this situation. Until then, don't say a word."

"You could talk to your mom. And I might be able to put my hands on Gigi's old journals," Maggie said. Jesi rolled her eyes. Jesi's mom was less involved with the coven than Jesi and she'd had a power for years. She just ignored hers. Jesi's was harder to ignore.

"Journals first, Mom later." Jesi picked up another book. "You know she doesn't like to talk about magic. But you're right. I should call her."

"Oh, here is something else about complements."

"Really?" Jesi stood and looked over Maggie's shoulder as she pointed to the start of the section.

"Maggie, you are the best."

"I know," Maggie said, smiling. "Here it says that the witch's active power cannot affect a witch's complement, which we knew. Once a witch meets his or her complement, the complement will see past the magic veil. Complements are a witch's match. They usually stay with the witch for life, either as a friend or lover. And in the case of Jesi Osman, her complement will be her lover." Maggie rolled the r as she said the word lover. Jesi whacked her on the shoulder.

"Okay, let me see that." Jesi took the book from Maggie and started reading through the passage. Jesi just began to feel confident using her power, like she could get her life back together. A complement would derail her progress. Right?

"Do you think there is a section that details how to tell someone that they are a complement and that magic is real?" Jesi asked, frowning at the text.

"Well, you can ask around the family on the 'magic is real' part. Only a handful are married to other witches."

"And no complements?"

"Nope. Just Gigi and Gramps." Maggie looked at Jesi. "So, technically he could be a witch, too, like Gramps. And you are each other's complement. So, let's talk about the part where you gave him your number."

"No, I gave him my card. In a professional manner. And what's the likelihood of a cop you don't know walking in here?"

"Slim to none," Maggie said. "You know I don't do well with cops. You should call him, though. At the station. Wine and dine him. Show him a magical time and get the scoop on the kid's disappearances."

"I think not. You've been here pouring over the volumes. Any idea where those two kids are?"

"Nope. But I know the kidnapper is magical. Once the first kid was taken, everyone in the coven placed protection spells around their houses and children. Whoever, or whatever, took them knows magic."

"Do you think they're in the community?"

"No. I don't. But some people do. It's causing some rifts," Maggie said.

"Who around here isn't a part of the coven?" Jesi asked. She only knew the witches associated with their coven, even the ones who lived a hundred miles out.

"You'd be surprised," Maggie said.

The bells on the door rang as a customer entered the shop. Jesi's eyes widened, and she dropped to the floor, sitting behind the counter. Maggie looked down at her. Jesi just shook her head, putting her finger to her lips. She hoped Maggie would play it cool. She was a little unpredictable. The last thing Jesi wanted was to visit with Detective Hottie right now.

"Hi. Welcome to Herbs and Healing of Savannah," Maggie said.

"Hi. I'm Detective Chuck Massey," he said. Jesi could hear the old counter creak under his weight as he leaned on it.

"Hi, I'm Margaret Watkins," Maggie said. "You can call me Maggie."

"I'm looking for someone. Do you think you could

help me?" His deep voice floated down, giving Jesi shivers behind the counter. From Jesi's seat, she could see Maggie's smile widen.

"Yes," Maggie said. Jesi heard Maggie as she mumbled a spell under her breath followed by Maggie yelling "REVEAL."

Jesi imagined Maggie throwing herbs at the detective. Some of them floated down on top of Jesi's head. He would arrest Maggie; she just knew it. Maggie performed this spell on several occasions. She liked to keep that combination of herbs on hand to reveal possessed, magical, or other customers. Jesi buried her head into her knees.

"Thank you for the handful of... potpourri," he said. "I'm looking for a Jessica Osman. I believe she works here."

"Really?" Maggie said more to herself.

"She doesn't work here?"

"Oh yes, she works here." Jesi hit Maggie's shin from under the counter. "She's not here right now."

"Well, she left her jacket at the station earlier." Jesi could see the edge of a cardigan draped over the counter next to the cash register. "Also, if she could call me? I have a few questions for someone posing as a lawyer in order to get information regarding an active case. I believe it constitutes as fraud."

Jesi heard him tap the counter and move. Posing as a lawyer? Who did he think he was? Jesi jumped up from behind the counter, red in the face.

"I am a lawyer. With an active license. I have every

right to question the progress of the police department on behalf of my clients."

The detective smiled. "I spoke with the people at Goldstein, Moore, and Smith. I hear you took a leave of absence a year ago. Why exactly do you work here?"

Jesi looked at Maggie and then back at the detective, switching from one foot to the other. "I'm helping my family while freelancing. Family comes first."

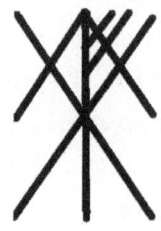

Chapter 2

Chuck looked at Jesi Osman as she stood with her head held high across the counter. She didn't exactly look like the family that owned this shop. He remembered Mrs. Oblena Watkins. She always sent work to his father's auto shop. And he'd seen Maggie Watkins at the shop as well. She's Mrs. Watkin's granddaughter, if he remembered correctly. Mrs. Watkins used to joke about being so white, she glowed in the moonlight. Jesi Osman was a lovely shade of brown, quite the opposite of Mrs. Watkins. And her black hair was pulled tight into a ponytail that ended with a puff of curls, like a rabbit's cottontail. He knew she was a lawyer, and he baited her out of hiding by poking at her pride. He spent the time to look her up after she ran from the station. There was something about the way she walked out that made him want to find out more. That and the fact that she latched onto his hand like she was afraid to let go. Was it to find out if she was connected to the case or just for her? He wasn't sure at the moment. Did she know more than she was letting on? The families of the missing children were holding back something. That he knew. Maybe Jesi Osman could help. His gut said it would be worth it either way.

"Family, huh?" he said, leaning back on the counter.

"If you must know, Detective Massey," Maggie said, "we're cousins. I needed help after our Gigi passed, and Jesi was nice enough to put her career on hold to help. This store has been in the family for decades."

He could hear Maggie tap her fingers on the counter. There was a hint of truth to the lie that passed from her lips. Jesi worked here, but not because of the death of Mrs. Watkins. Chuck kept his eyes on Jesi. She had answers he needed. She bit her bottom lip, but kept eye contact. And Chuck could get lost in those dark blue eyes.

"Please, call me Chuck," he said. "Ms. Osman, is there anywhere we can talk more privately?" Jesi looked around the shop as she rubbed her hands down the side of her legs.

"You can use the 'Employees Only' room." Maggie pointed to a room toward the back of the store. The door was ajar, and the light was on.

"That door says 'The Magic Room'," he said.

Maggie nudged Jesi, whose eyes widened to the size of saucers.

"So, it does," Maggie said. "Just don't touch anything."

"If you'll excuse us," Jesi said as she pulled Maggie

away from the counter and into the open room behind them.

Chuck leaned in, trying to eavesdrop. He heard small hisses and sharp t's at the ends of words as Jesi waved her arms, talking to Maggie. He straightened up as they both came out of the room.

Jesi motioned for them to move to 'The Magic Room'. The room was much larger than the storage closet he expected. It had shelves similar to the main store. The labels here were color coded and bold. Unrecognizable symbols danced on the labels beside the names. Jesi closed the door behind them. Chuck looked at a bin marked 'Feathers of Grace'. He picked one up. The color changed in the light as he turned it.

"Don't touch that," Jesi said as she snatched it out of his hand and put it back.

"What?" he asked. "Why?"

He watched Jesi as she sighed and opened and closed her mouth before saying, "It's... well, it's magic. And dangerous."

"Magic isn't real," he said with a sigh. He didn't have time for fairy tales. He questioned his motivation for following her here. Maybe she came to work here because of a meltdown.

"If it were only so easy," Jesi said. She walked to the door and pushed it open quickly. Chuck peered around Jesi to see Maggie on the ground. Eavesdropper. Jesi's hands were on her hips. She shook her head at Maggie and shut the door.

"Magic is very real," Jesi said, turning toward Chuck.

"No one wishes it was a fantasy more than me."

"And why is that?" he asked.

She looked at the ground. Her arms crossed over her chest. "That's a long story that I'm not ready to tell, Detective." She looked up. Her dark blue eyes peered into his. "What exactly do you want to talk to me about?"

Chuck lost himself in those eyes. Why did he track her down again? Why was she at the station? "The kids," he said. "You have a connection with the two families. What exactly did you hope to learn from your visit? And, please, call me Chuck."

"Well, Chuck, I wanted to know if there was any recent information," Jesi said as she glanced around the room. "The parents are going crazy. Nothing we've tried has helped us find their children."

"This is a police investigation. It should not involve you. Any movement on your part can destroy any progress the department has made. What have you done exactly?"

"Frankly, we have resources that the police don't have," Jesi said, "and our resources are revealing nothing. We're at a dead end. We could use your help. We hoped that you would have better leads and, I don't know, maybe we could work together."

"What resources?" Chuck looked down at Jesi. She lifted her head high.

"Of the magical kind," Jesi said. "That's all you need to know."

"I would like to know the specifics," Chuck said between his teeth. Outside involvement was nothing he took lightly. People had died from it. He watched as she bit her lip and took a deep breath.

"We've tried everything from scrying and tracking spells to enlisting the local werewolf pack to sniff them out."

Chuck stared at Jesi. He must have stepped into the nuthouse. He really should leave or arrest her for interfering in an active investigation, but something tugged at the back of his mind. That spark when they first touched. Was it more than just static electricity?

"Werewolf pack?" he heard himself saying. He rolled his eyes for even entertaining the notion.

"Please, don't go telling anyone and everyone," Jesi said. "I just feel like I can trust you. And I need you to trust me. I can help you find those kids. I mean, we can. Maggie and I."

"You are going to have to give me more than just your word on magic. It's pretty unbelievable. I can't put it in a report."

Jesi looked around the room. She grabbed a small rock from the wall beside the door. Holding it up for him to see, she closed her eyes and began taking deep breaths. She suddenly opened her eyes and said, "Rock of the ground, worm out and around."

The rock in her hand glowed. Then it flattened to half its height and uncurled. An earthworm wiggled where the rock once sat.

Chuck's mouth hung open. His mother's voice echoed in his head, telling him that flies were going to fly inside his mouth. But this wasn't like watching a baseball game or a shuttle launch. Nothing he could tell himself could get him to close it. Jesi took a few steps forward.

"Do you want to hold it?" Jesi asked.

Chuck stared at the worm in Jesi's hand. He was aware of her biting her lip and moving her weight from foot to foot. He took a shaky breath and held out his hand. The worm wiggled around when she gave it to him, and it almost fell to the floor. Between the worm and her lips, he was a little distracted. He let it move through his fingers. He felt the worm as it wiggled. Then he sniffed it. It looked, felt, and smelled like an earthworm. If he had a pole, he'd go fishing.

"How long will this last?" he asked in a whisper.

"Forever, or until I change it back."

"Is it always that easy?" Chuck looked at her. Her frown was deep. His mouth was still gaping.

"No. The rocks in here are charged or energized with magical, uh, energy. That's why it's in this room. I would need a longer spell if it was an uncharged rock."

"Can you change it back? In my hand?" Chuck wanted to feel the magic, to see if he could feel the magic. Maybe he was having a stroke or hallucinating. It was the obvious explanation. As Jesi touched his hand to position it, static warmth tingled down his arm. They stopped and stared at each other. Chuck could hear her heart beating. Or maybe it was his.

Jesi shook her head and moved his hand so his palm pointed upward with the worm in the middle. She took a deep breath. "What was done, now undo, return the worm to the rock that's true."

The worm wiggled and curled in on itself. It glowed again. A soft blue glow. Its size doubled and hardened. Just as quickly as before, it was a rock. Chuck turned it over in his shaking hand. He smelled it.

"Does it still smell like a worm?" Jesi asked.

"No. Just like a rock." Chuck's eyes were wide. He looked at the rock, then at Jesi, and back at the rock.

"Good," Jesi smiled. "The last few times I've tried, the smell lingered."

"So... magic," Chuck said. He stared at the rock. His heart beat hard in his chest.

"Yeah. Magic."

"I have to go," Chuck said. He squeezed the rock in his hand. The pain helped him focus, but he needed to leave this crazy place. He was hallucinating. It must be something from the potpourri Ms. Maggie Watkins put in his hand. He backed up and bumped into the door. Jesi frowned at him. He searched for the doorknob behind him with his free hand.

"I know this is a lot to take in, but I really think you should stay, and we can talk about it." Jesi held out a hand in front of her and inched toward him.

Couldn't she see he wasn't a dumb dog she could coax into submission? He finally found the knob and fumbled out the door. With urgency, he walked toward the entrance. He didn't look back at Ms. Watkins. He didn't look back at Jesi. He made it out the door with a loud clang of the bells behind him. Inside his car with the rock still clutched in his hand, he thought of the one person he could trust, and he started the car.

~

Jesi stared at the door as it banged shut. The bells clashed loudly inside the shop.

"So," Maggie said, "he take it well?"

"Not exactly," Jesi said. "I guess we need to put together that amnesia spell."

"Nah," Maggie said. "He'll be back. I've got a good feeling about him."

Jesi turned and looked at her cousin. "I'm going to go look for that spell, anyway."

"Do what you want," Maggie said, "but don't take too long. Finding the kids takes priority."

While Maggie thought she was an excellent judge of character, Jesi was good at covering every angle. That made her an excellent lawyer. And today, she would channel that energy into the spell to keep the detective from exposing the supernatural.

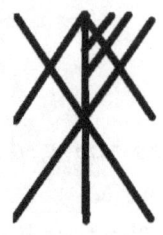

Chapter 3

Chuck made his way over to his father's auto shop. Alan Massey was Chuck's father in all the ways that mattered. He learned in high school that Alan wasn't his biological father, but it didn't change how Chuck felt. Alan was his dad and would always be the best person to talk to when things got rough. Today was one of those days.

Chuck pulled up to the shop. The Massey and Sons Automotive sign stood tall in front of the building. It was the best shop in Southside, Savannah, according to a local paper. Chuck remembered the time he told his dad he didn't want to be a mechanic, that he wanted to be a police officer. Chuck knew his dad hoped his kids would take over one day. He expected his dad to be furious and disappointed. He just pulled Chuck into the biggest hug and said, "No matter what you do, I'll be proud of you."

Chuck walked into the small shop and was greeted by his dad. The front waiting room held four chairs and a desk. A small hallway behind the desk led to a bathroom and an office where his dad did all the paperwork. He tried to teach Chuck, at one point, how to do all the office work, but that did not last long.

"Hey, son," his dad said while filling out a form.

"Hey," Chuck said. "Do you have time to talk?"

"To my son, the detective?" He smiled and put down his pen. "Always. Let's go to the office."

Chuck closed the door after they entered the small office. He took a seat to find his dad looking at him with a raised eyebrow. "Must be serious if you're closing the door."

"It's private," Chuck said. He tried to think of a way to talk about what just happened while he looked around the familiar room. His dad sat behind a desk with an old computer monitor to one side. Papers and manuals covered the rest of the desk. The walls held old auto parts posters that his father found funny. Behind his father's head hung the licenses for the business and certifications his father thought most important. He had his sister's certification displayed as well.

"You just missed your sister."

Chuck thought his dad could come up with a better way to break the tension.

"Did she bring 'him' with her?" Chuck asked. His sister, Hayley, was currently seeing someone Chuck despised. Their parents disliked the guy themselves.

"Unfortunately," his dad said with a deep frown. "She dropped off his car to get it worked on. An oil change and new brakes."

"What?" Chuck said too loud. "She can do that

herself. She even has the tools."

"I know." He shook his head. "I told her she could do it herself and even use a bay here. 'He' said that she had better things to do."

"And now he's talking for her." Chuck sat back in the chair. "What has she gotten herself into?"

"I don't want to cause you any more frustration, but I thought you should know the latest with your sister," he said. "So, let's change gears. What's on your mind, Chuck?"

"Well, I've had a strange morning," Chuck said. He stuck his hand in his pocket and grabbed the rock. Jesi asked him not to tell anyone, but he needed a different perspective. He trusted his father more than anyone and he gave rational, calm advice.

"How so?"

"I'm working on this case with the missing children. I'm sure you've seen it on the news. Anyway, I may have a lead. But the lead is crazy. Or I'm crazy. Or going crazy." Chuck shook his head.

"Define 'crazy'."

"My potential lead... um... she thinks she's a witch."

Alan's eyes got wide. "What's this young lady's name?"

"Jesi. Jesi Osman."

His dad shook his head. "That name doesn't sound familiar. Why does she think she's a witch and why is that crazy? I hear Wicca is very popular."

"Well, she is a lawyer, but she left her job to help her cousin at that herb shop near Forsyth Park and I'm starting to think she is not crazy. That maybe she is a witch."

"Is that Oblena Watkin's old shop?" his father asked.

"Yeah," Chuck said. "And what if magic is real? None of this makes sense. I shouldn't even be telling you any of this. I mean, if magic is real, how am I supposed to do my job? How can I investigate something if it's tampered with magically? And then it brings up whether magic is inherently good or bad? And are there other magical creatures, or should I just go see a neurologist?" Chuck put his head in his hands. "The thing is, I believe her and everything she's told me. She turned this rock into a worm right before my eyes." Chuck held up the rock to his dad.

"What's the cousin's name?" his father asked.

"Did you hear what I said?" Chuck asked. "What does it matter?"

"Just indulge me." He smirked at Chuck.

"Um, Maggie Watkins." Chuck frowned back at his dad.

"That's right." His dad rubbed his chin. "Maggie took over when Oblena died."

"Yeah, I guess," Chuck said with a shrug. "I've seen her here before."

"Yeah. She gets her car worked on here. The entire coven does. The supernatural community trust this shop."

"What?" Chuck asked. "Supernatural community?"

"Yes." His dad leaned forward and put his elbows on his knees and looked Chuck straight in the eyes. "Now, everything I'm about to tell you can't leave this room. As in, you can't talk about this at your office or with your sister. I hate to break it to you, but magic is very real. I have a couple of werewolves working here. Great workers. They just need extra time off three nights a month."

"Three nights?" Chuck closed his eyes and massaged his temples. "You know, let's come back to that. Why am I just hearing about this?"

"Son, you've always seen things in a black and white way," he said. "Things were good or bad. And you wanted to be a cop since you were little. I didn't know how to tell you that some things were gray and existed outside the law. There are some things you can't arrest and some things that don't need arresting. Some seem scary, but they aren't bad."

"Are you saying they are trustworthy?" Chuck could hardly believe what his father said.

"The wolves who work here?" he asked. "Sure. I'd trust them with my life. That doesn't mean there aren't bad ones. Just like everything else in this life, some are good, some are bad, and some are in a bad spot."

Chuck nodded his head at his dad's words. "And Hayley doesn't know?"

"No." His father sighed. "I was going to tell her. Then Roger showed up. Suddenly, nothing I said meant anything. She thinks I've been lying to her, about anything and everything." Chuck shook his head. He really hated that Roger, but Chuck couldn't find anything on him.

"And all the wolves here say he smells bad. It worries

me," he said.

"Bad how?" Chuck lifted an eyebrow.

"Just bad. Like bad magic one of them said." The lines on his dad's forehead deepened.

"What does that even mean?" Chuck asked. His dad shrugged his shoulders and leaned back in his chair. Chuck leaned back as well and scrubbed his face with his hands again. He looked at the ceiling and hoped something would cause the world to make sense again. "How long have you known about the supernatural?" Chuck asked.

"Since I was eighteen," he said. "A werewolf bit my best friend and turned him into one. It's another long story, at least a story for another time."

"Isaiah is a werewolf? I wonder how many other people I know that are supernatural." Chuck sat forward on the chair with his elbows on his knees and stared at the wall. "I think these two witches at that shop can help with my case. Is it crazy to consider that?"

"I've known Oblena since I was twenty years old," his dad said. "I'd trust her with my life. And I've always had a good feeling about Maggie. And the wolves here say nothing but good things about her. Of course, you decide for yourself."

"What about Jesi?" Chuck asked. He straightened his back.

"I don't recall the name," he said. "You're on your own there, but you have a good gut. Listen to it."

"Thanks, Dad," Chuck said. His father came over to him and slapped him on the back.

As he walked through the door, he called back, "Oh, and your sister got a tattoo." Chuck looked up at his father, slack jawed. "It's awful," his dad said, then left Chuck there to think things over.

~

Chuck drove back to the building that housed Herbs and Healing. It was a two-story brick building that looked like an old home. The front held a porch the length of the building with columns from floor to ceiling. Flower beds bloomed with early spring flowers on either side of the steps, and he nodded in approval of the handicap ramp addition leading to the side of the porch. He didn't plan to come back, but the talk with his dad eased his mind. His heart pounded as he opened the door once more.

Jesi talked to an older gentleman in front of the counter. Maggie sat on the other side of the counter with a woman he didn't recognize. Probably another witch, he thought to himself. She was taller than the other two, with light brown hair. She didn't seem too interested in his arrival.

Jesi only glanced up at him once while she spoke to the old man. She put the stack of papers she was showing him into a manilla folder and handed it to him. The old man smiled at her and moved in to kiss her on the cheek. Jesi took a quick step back.

"Oh, I remember," the man said. He touched the side of his nose with a smile.

"It's no problem," Jesi said. "Don't forget to take that

to the clerk's office today. Are you sure you don't want me to take it?"

"I'm sure," he said. "Have a nice day now. Bye Maggie, Emma." He turned, nodded at Chuck, and left the store.

"Ms. Osman," Chuck said. "May I have another word with you?"

Jesi looked to Maggie. He saw Maggie give a quick, wide-eyed nod. "Yes, shall we go to the Magic Room again?"

Chuck nodded and followed her once again into the small side room. He closed the door behind him and paced a bit before stopping.

"Who was that man you were talking to?" Chuck asked. He knew it wasn't his business, but he couldn't stop himself from asking.

"That was Pete Chambers," Jesi said. "I drew up some legal papers for him. It keeps me from getting rusty and I don't mind helping the, ah, community."

He nodded as he thought about how to phrase his question. "So, just for a moment, let's say magic is real. What does it have to do with the two missing children?" He focused on breathing slower. He stuck his hand in his pocket to feel the rock.

"Are you sure you're ready for this?" Jesi asked. Her eyebrows lifted and her eyes stared into his.

"Yes," he said with a big breath. "What does magic have to do with the children?"

"They are both active witches." Jesi stood still and rigid. Her eyes focused solely on him.

"What do you mean, active witches?" Chuck asked.

"Active witches have a power specific to themselves. It is something we can just do, an instinctive ability. Like grow a plant or predict the weather with pinpoint accuracy."

"How do you know they have active powers?" Chuck shook his head. Jesi rubbed the sides of her legs.

"We—I—there is a group of us, and we keep tabs on each other," she answered.

"And you all have active powers?" he asked. "How many are there?"

"I don't know the exact number," she said. "And no, not everyone has active powers. Some married witches or some are born to a family and never received a witch power. If those without a power want to do magic, they have to do it the extra-long way. Cast a circle, use herbs or crystals, or, well, Maggie can explain that better."

"What's your active power?" he asked. He took a step closer.

Jesi looked around the room. "Well," she said after a long pause, "I can see someone's past with a touch."

Chuck's eyes widened. "The past? Like everything?"

Jesi nodded. "Up to the minute before I touch them. It's called gleaning. To glean."

"Everyone you touch?" His voice came out higher than normal.

"Um…" Jesi chewed her lip. "I can't glean you. I mean, when I touched you, I saw nothing."

"Really?" Chuck rubbed his chin and held tighter to the rock in his pocket with his other hand. "You shook hands with Detective Thompson today. Can you tell me something about him?"

"Great, twenty questions." Jesi rolled her eyes. "He puts more sugar than coffee in his coffee."

"Too easy." It would not fool Chuck. He'd heard how the psychic scene worked. As much as his gut told him to trust her, his brain wasn't so sure.

"Okay," Jesi sighed. "He told you yesterday that he didn't want to work on the missing kids' case, because he doesn't like kids and they probably just ran away."

"Yeah, he's a real piece of work." Chuck squinted his eyes and frowned. No one was around when Chuck had that conversation with Thompson. Was it just a guess? No, his father verified magic, but he knew he would do a sweep for bugs later. "And you picked up nothing from me?"

"Oh, I'm picking up something, just not magically," Jesi said with a smile.

"Must be chemistry then." Chuck returned her smile. Was she flirting? It was the last thing he expected and the last thing he should encourage but, in that moment, it all felt so easy. A phone rang. It sounded like an old rotary phone.

"We can talk about that later." Jesi turned to leave the room. Chuck blocked her path. He wrapped his hand around hers. The static warmed his arm again. He looked into her eyes.

"I'll hold you to it," he said with half a smile. She smiled back and walked through the door.

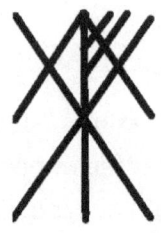

Chapter 4

Jesi walked out of the Magic Room with Chuck in tow.

Maggie answered the phone that hung behind the counter. It was an old phone wired into the wall; technology a step newer than a rotary phone, even though it still sounded like a rotary. They called it the Witch Line. It was the number anyone in the coven called when something important was happening. Maggie was given the title of 'Witch Line Operator' when she inherited the shop. While she argued against it, Jesi couldn't think of anyone better suited for the job.

"This is Maggie," Maggie said as they approached the counter.

On the other side of the counter with Maggie, stood Maggie's best friend, Emma Luvel. Jesi saw her at least once a week, if not more. She came to talk or help, usually around closing. She was a veterinarian and worked on the other side of town.

"Hi, I'm Emma," she said with a smile. "You must be

the Detective Massey Maggie told me about."

Chuck shook hands with Emma. "Please, call me Chuck."

"What? Yes, of course. We'll be right over," Maggie said into the phone.

"So, Detective Chuck, are you arresting our Jesi today?" Emma asked while she smiled. Her wide smile showed an impossible amount of teeth. The canines were prominent and pointy. Her smile made people uncomfortable. Chuck gave Jesi a side glance. Jesi shrugged.

"Not today," Chuck said. "Have we met? You look familiar."

"It's possible," Emma said.

"Okay, I'll see you soon," Maggie said as she slammed down the receiver. "Let's go, Jesi." Maggie rummaged under the counter. "We're closing up shop for a bit, people. Everyone out."

"Right now?" Jesi asked. She did a slight side nod toward Chuck.

"Judy Nelson called. Something happened at Genevieve's house. They might have some information. Your kind of information."

Jesi took in a quick breath of air and rushed to get her stuff together. Judy Nelson, the mother of Pattie Nelson, the second child kidnapped. Jesi didn't like being asked to use her power, even if she knew the importance. And her power failed her once today. Her heart rate rose. She shook off some of her anxiety.

"Nice cover, but this cardigan isn't mine." Jesi

handed him the cardigan. Jesi shook her head at him and pulled her bag on her shoulder.

"Worth it," Chuck said with a smile. Jesi smiled back despite herself. She turned away to hide her blushing cheeks. He turned to Maggie. "What happened? Maybe I can help."

Jesi looked from Chuck back to Maggie. Maggie raised an eyebrow. "He seems to be coming around on the magic thing," Jesi said with a scrunched-up face.

Maggie tapped her fingers on the counter. "We may have a lead. Jesi will call you if it pans out."

"What kind of lead?" Chuck asked.

Jesi didn't move. Maggie put her hands on her hips and raised her head to look Chuck in the eyes.

"We will call you if we need you," Maggie said.

"You tell me what is happening, and I will make that decision." Chuck stared back at Maggie.

Jesi's eyes widened. It felt like two titans facing down each other. "If it involves Judy Nelson, I need to be there."

Maggie broke eye contact first. "Damn it." She flung her arms in the air. "Fine. There was an attempt to take an eight-year-old girl. Judy thinks it's related to her daughter's kidnapping."

"And they haven't called the cops?" Chuck asked.

"No offense, but if we can figure this out, we don't need the cops." Maggie headed toward the door and looked back only at Jesi.

Chuck and Emma brought up the rear. Once out the door, Jesi locked up and watched Emma walk away.

"Call me if you need a nose," Emma yelled over her

shoulder.

The rest of them followed Maggie to her car. Chuck opened the back door.

"What are you doing?" Maggie asked. Jesi stood still with her hand on the door handle.

"I'm coming with you." Chuck stared down at Maggie again.

"No."

"Yes. This is a police matter."

"It is when Genevieve calls the police. Until then, stay out of my car." Maggie's nostrils flared.

Detective Chuck stepped back and slammed the door.

"Maggie," Jesi said, dragging out the 'ie' in the name. Jesi looked at Maggie with raised eyebrows and motioned with her head toward Chuck. Jesi knew this was a perfect opportunity to create a bridge of trust with him. It was Maggie's idea to incorporate him into the investigation. She'd hate it when Jesi pointed it out, especially since Maggie wasn't the biggest fan of the police.

"Really? You want him to go?"

"I think it is a good idea." Jesi stood up straighter and pulled down her blazer.

"Is this because of the thing?" Maggie frowned at Jesi.

"Uh. Yeah. And because of what you said about cooperation."

Maggie rolled her eyes. "I didn't think it would involve me. He's a cop."

Jesi continued to stare at Maggie. Jesi knew Maggie

only wanted to work with the cops on her terms. Jesi hoped her eyes looked pleading enough.

"Fine. Detective, you're back in." Maggie dropped into the car with a huff. Jesi sat in the front seat and Chuck sat behind Maggie. Jesi wondered if this was a bad idea as the car started.

~

Maggie drove toward Genevieve's place, with Jesi stealing quick glances at Chuck. He would be lying if he wasn't stealing his own glances. It was the reason he was sitting behind Maggie; he wanted a better look at Jesi. He wasn't sure what exactly was happening, but he didn't want to miss it. Something about Jesi, um, the magic, he reminded himself, the magic that had him tagging along.

"Soooo, Detective Chuck," Maggie said. "Can I call you Chuckers?"

"No," Chuck said. "Call me Chuck or Detective Massey."

"Great. So, Chuckers, why exactly didn't you take your own car?"

"I don't trust you enough to not try to lose me, or leave me behind."

"Smart. Okay, when we get to Genevieve's place, you need to understand what's going to happen," Maggie continued.

He grunted. Who exactly did she think she was? Jesi stared at Maggie with wide eyes, then turned and gave him a small smile. Chuck leaned back into the seat, making himself comfortable.

"They haven't called the police, so they will be distant. I'm not sure Genevieve will be comfortable with you showing up with us and she may ask you to leave. However, coming there with us is actually in your favor. But Jesi needs to do her thing. Let her work. Save your questions for the end." Maggie met Chuck's eyes through the rear-view mirror.

Chuck said nothing. He wanted to find the missing children. He breathed hard in and out of his nose. And try as he might, he couldn't stop his leg as it shook up and down. It was an old nervous habit.

He focused on Jesi. She turned her head toward the window during Maggie's warning. Her shoulders were tense. What exactly was Jesi going to do? Could she really see into someone's past?

"Okay?" Maggie asked.

"This really is a police matter," Chuck said. He wasn't happy about being bossed around, especially not by some purple haired hippy.

"The disappearances are a police matter. This may not be connected at all," Maggie said.

"That's not how that works. Children are in danger. We should treat this as if it's connected until we can rule it out. We should have forensics on the scene." He could hear his voice get louder as he talked. He needed to get control of himself.

"I know you're doing your job, but so are we. Jesi is vouching for you. I'm vouching for you. What you do here will reflect on us. Mostly her, but really us. Please, follow our lead."

"There is only so much following I will do. You are pressing the limits." His illusion of being relaxed vanished as he leaned toward the front seat.

"Chuck, please." Jesi looked back at him. "Maggie isn't usually so bossy. She's been around this more than you and knows how our people work. Please, trust us. You will get the information you need." Her eyes were so open in that moment, he couldn't pull himself out of them.

"Is this girl also an active witch?" Chuck asked.

"How much did you tell him?" Maggie gaped at Jesi.

Jesi shrugged. "Not everything. Besides, it's easier in the long run. Trust and all that."

Chuck looked at Jesi as she avoided eye contact. Not everything. What information was he missing?

"Geez Louise," Maggie said, shaking her head. "I can't believe you choose now to listen to me."

"I always listen to you," Jesi said. "I just don't always follow your advice."

"I just hoped you'd move slower," Maggie said.

"I just hope my gut is right about you," Chuck said. He glared at Jesi. Her blue eyes met his.

"Of course, it is. I'm lovable and trustworthy," Maggie said.

Chuck caught her wink at Jesi. Jesi rolled her eyes with a smile.

"And modest," Jesi said.

They pulled up to the house. It was a brick ranch on the southside of town. Most of the houses in this area were built in the 70s, and almost all of them were one story. The only other car at Genevieve's place belonged to Judy Nelson. Chuck recognized it as hers from his visit to her house after her daughter disappeared. They climbed out of the vehicle and made their way to the front door. The warm wind of late spring pushed past them. The faded blue door opened as they approached, and Judy rushed out to hug Maggie.

"Thank you so much for coming," she breathed.

"Of course," Maggie said.

She pulled back and looked behind Maggie at Chuck. Her eyes darkened. The worry lines on her face deepened.

"What's he doing here?" she asked sharply.

Chuck put on his sympathetic face, or at least what he thought his sympathetic face was. He wasn't sure what his face was doing after walking into the herb shop.

"Oh, him?" Maggie motioned at Chuck. "The detective here will tag along per Jesi's request."

"I don't know if Genevieve will like that."

"He's not here in any official police capacity. Isn't that right, Chuck?" she asked with an emphasis on the k.

"That is correct, Margaret." He ended on the hard 't'. Chuck could play this game. The trust that Judy gave Maggie was enough for him to keep his mouth shut for now. Judy took one last look at him and led them into the house.

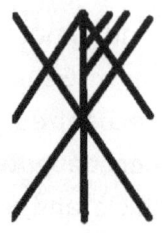

Chapter 5

Jesi looked around Genevieve's cozy house. She had herbs hanging over the kitchen island and pots on the stove. Light filtered in through the many windows in the back. Sage burned on the dining room table.

Genevieve was sitting on the couch wrapped around her daughter. They were both tall and slim, with matching dark brown hair that flowed together as if it shared the same source. Genevieve didn't move when she saw the group, content to rock Amber in her arms.

"Hey, Genevieve. Amber." Maggie kneeled next to them, rubbing an arm on each of them. Jesi thought she might bring them both in for a hug.

"Thank you for coming." Tears welled up in Genevieve's eyes.

"You know Jesi, right?" Maggie said as they both nodded. "And this is Jesi's friend, Chuck. You can call him Chuckers." Maggie winked at Amber with a big smile. Amber's mouth moved in a tiny upward trajectory. "Can you tell us what happened?"

Amber looked at her mom and back to the group, shrugging. Genevieve smoothed Amber's hair, glancing at Jesi and Chuck. Jesi felt the urge to give them both a giant hug.

"Are you sure it's safe to have him here?" Genevieve tried to whisper, but everyone could hear her.

Jesi understood. This was coven business until it wasn't. Maggie looked back at Jesi with raised eyebrows. It was Jesi's decision to have him here. And if they didn't want to talk in front of Chuck, he would have to leave. That thought tugged at her heart. She bit her lip and looked at Chuck, then moved toward the group on the couch.

"Please, trust my judgement," Jesi said. "He is one of the special ones." Jesi wasn't sure where that thought came from. If he was her complement, then he would be a special one. "But if you want him to leave, he will."

Jesi looked back at Chuck. He nodded.

"Okay," Genevieve said. "Sweetie, please, tell Maggie and Jesi about what happened."

"Are you sure?" Amber's small voice came out as a squeak.

Her mom nodded while petting Amber's hair. Amber turned to the group and sat up straight on the couch.

"Anytime you're ready," Maggie said to Amber and patted her legs.

She breathed in and out slowly.

"I was in my room playing. And hands grabbed me from behind. I screamed and fought him off." She looked at her mom. Genevieve nodded. "I burned him pretty bad."

Maggie held Amber's hands. "Where did you burn him?"

"On the back of his hands or wrist and more on his sides, I think." Amber pointed out the areas on her hands.

"You did great. Now, you know Jesi, right?" Maggie asked. Amber nodded. "Well, Jesi needs to hold your hands for a while, okay?"

"Okay."

Maggie let go of Amber's hands and nodded at Jesi. Jesi positioned herself beside Amber on the couch and held her hand out to Amber. Jesi took a deep breath as Amber put her hands in Jesi's.

In an instant, Amber's life flashed before Jesi's eyes. She breathed hard as the memories fluttered through her mind. *Focus, Jesi*, she told herself as she filtered the girl's life.

According to Gigi's notes, shorter lives were easier to wade through. Jesi wasn't so sure about that. While she no longer felt like she was drowning with each touch, young or old, it was still a shock to her system. Normally, she could go through the memories slowly after the touch happened. Only the big memories stuck with her right away. Here, she would need to look for the memories while she was holding Amber. It made the experience more intense.

Jesi looked for the last few hours of Amber's life. The memories flickered and slowed like an old movie reel. She could see the dark figure and felt hands on her stomach.

Amber acted on instinct. She grabbed the hands and burned the flesh off. They threw her across the room. Her head jerked up, getting one good look at him. Yes. A man. Jesi slowed it down more. He had his hood up, but he was a white male with dark hair and a five o'clock shadow. He was holding his hands, charred and bleeding. His eyes flashed red before he turned and left in a pool of smoke.

Jesi let go of Amber's hand, only to grab her back into a hug.

"That's it?" Amber asked.

"That's it," Jesi said.

"Did you really see everything? It was only five seconds," Amber said. "I counted."

"Yes," Jesi said, "And you were so brave. I'm so proud of you."

"Normally Jesi doesn't need to hold on for so long," Maggie said.

"That's true," Jesi said with a glance at Maggie, "but it takes longer to process a person's life if I only touch someone for a second." Jesi resisted the urge to give Maggie a dirty look. The explanation wasn't something everyone needed.

"Genevieve, Amber," Maggie said. "Would it be okay if the three of us go to Amber's room and look around?"

Jesi looked at the detective, who remained standing. His eyes bored into hers with a tight smile and a lifted eyebrow. She could only guess what she looked like to him right now. She smoothed down her hair and pulled down her blazer when she stood. She felt out of sorts from the length of the contact with Amber.

"Of course," Jesi heard Genevieve say.

Jesi jerked her head toward the hallway and headed that way, feeling him behind her. The three of them entered Amber's room. Jesi just stood in the middle and looked around.

Her room was what she expected from an eight-year-old. The light green walls and white furniture were reminiscent of adolescence. Stuffed animals filled the corners, and pictures of animals and kid stars hung on the walls. There was makeup on her mirrored dresser and forest animal curtains over the windows. The level of innocence the intruder took away from Amber stirred an anger inside Jesi she never felt before.

She watched Chuck to distract her from the anger building up inside. He used a pen to lift and move papers and fabric around. He took out his flashlight to inspect under the bed and the windowsill. His method was slow and methodical. Nothing seemed to escape his inspection, including her. Every few minutes, he would glance in her direction. She didn't bother to look away. As he finished looking through the last corner, Maggie nudged her.

"So, Jesi," Maggie said. "Can you walk us through what happened and where?"

"Yeah." Jesi glanced again at Chuck and moved toward the bed.

"So, Amber was kneeling here, facing the nightstand, playing with headphones and a stuffed animal, when she was grabbed from behind." Jesi demonstrated Amber's position in front of the nightstand. She frowned as she went through the footsteps of Amber.

"Where was she grabbed?" Chuck asked.

"Here, around her waist." Jesi put her hands on her stomach where she remembered the sensation from the connection with Amber. "Amber gasped and put her hands over his hands. Then her power activated. She burned the backs of his hands."

"Is this the first time Amber has used heat or fire?" Maggie asked.

Jesi thought Maggie should have asked Amber that herself. Jesi closed her eyes and looked through Amber's life.

"No. She could heat up cups of coffee and tea for about 3 years now. But not fire. Although, I'm pretty sure she used fire on her intruder." Jesi felt the sensations in her hands when she thought about it.

"Okay," Chuck drawled. "And then what happened?"

"He threw her over here." Jesi moved over to the opposite end of the room where a broken toy box sat. "She turned and looked up at the guy."

Chuck wrote in the little notebook she assumed all cops use. His hair fell almost in his eyes and his tongue stuck out a little to the right of his mouth. Jesi sensed a sudden urge to lick that side of his mouth. She shook her head. This was not the time or the place. She glanced back at Maggie, who looked at her with a raised eyebrow. Okay, she was busted.

"His hair is dark," Jesi said. "Either black or dark brown. He had a hoodie on with the hood up that hid the features of his face. Though I could tell he was unshaven and when Amber looked at him, his eyes flashed red."

Chills ran up her spine as she remembered the look in his eyes. She hugged her arms around her waist.

"Red?" Chuck asked. Now, he had an eyebrow raised.

"Yes," Jesi said, dragging out the 's' sound at the end. She stood up straighter and stared back at him.

"Okay, so Amber said he disappeared. Tell us about that." Maggie brought Jesi back to the task at hand.

Jesi almost questioned Chuck's trust of her. They had only known each other for a few hours. She knew what she felt was irrational.

"Uh, he turned and jumped out of the window, turning into smoke or leaving smoke? And he didn't just jump. He crouched all the way down to the ground and then jumped. It's possible he used a potion bag or something else to create the effect." Jesi walked over to where he was standing when he jumped.

"Here." She stood in the spot and showed the jump.

Maggie walked over and got on her hands and knees, inspecting the carpet at her feet. Chuck did the same.

Jesi stepped over the two, making her way to the door. Jesi didn't know what they were looking for. She never paid attention to her magic lessons growing up, and when an active power didn't manifest, she was perfectly happy to skip the rest. The past year proved difficult. She played catch up on years of forgotten or unlearned knowledge. She didn't know where she would be without Maggie's help.

"Jesi," Maggie said, "can you get me a small jar out of my bag by the door?"

Jesi obliged and brought it over. Jesi watched as Maggie scooped a tiny amount of something into the vial. The dark material was almost unnoticeable, but Chuck pulled out a small paper pouch marked 'EVIDENCE' and used it to gather the same substance.

"What do you think this is?" Chuck looked up at Maggie as she closed her bottle.

"Don't know. It wasn't on the window or the sill. I haven't seen it anywhere else. It might take me some time to identify it." She placed the vial in her pocket. "Do you have any ideas?"

"Not at the moment." He placed his now sealed pouch back in his pocket as well.

"Is there anything else we need to do?" Jesi asked, although she didn't know who she was asking.

"I'm going to talk to Genevieve about monitoring Amber. Then go back to the shop to identify the mystery substance," Maggie said as she looked from Jesi back to Chuck.

"I'm going to figure out how to get this processed without having it assigned to a case." Chuck eyed Jesi. "I'm putting myself at risk for you." He pulled out his phone and looked at it. "I've got to go." Then he walked out of the room and headed toward the living room. They could hear him say goodbye to Genevieve.

"I think he forgot we're his ride." Maggie gave Jesi a big smile and did her happy skip-step out of the room and down the hall with Jesi following. Jesi smiled, but her thoughts were somewhere between flashing red eyes and a handsome detective.

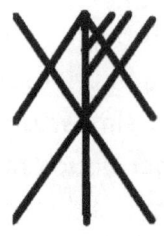

Chapter 6

Jesi watched Maggie talk to Sylvia on the phone.

Sylvia became the coven leader after Gigi passed. She was Gigi's oldest granddaughter, and the most trusted witch in the coven. Jesi stopped calling her Aunt Sylvia long ago. Sylvia never approved of how Jesi's mother raised her. Jesi's mom took her husband's name and didn't force Jesi to study witchcraft. And sometimes, she took Jesi away on long trips instead of staying for the high holidays like Beltane or Mabon. When Jesi didn't develop a power by puberty, Jesi's mom said she was free. Jesi could do whatever she wanted. That included moving far away. There were no expectations for Jesi anymore, and her mom liked that.

Her mom never appreciated having her own life planned out. Who would? She had planned to move away, but fell in love with a local boy who stayed in the area. Jesi was born of their love and, without an active power, she pursued law. She wanted to right wrongs and keep the innocent safe. It was impossible now that she knew when a client lied or when the opposing council twisted the truth. While she often suspected her co-workers or clients lied, it became an enormous distraction at work when she knew with absolute certainty. Every touch came with a backstory. And lawyers shook everyone's hands. And everyone's memories in the corporate law world were ripe with actions that turned Jesi's stomach. It proved to be too much for her.

So, she quit and trained with Maggie for the past year. Maggie never seemed to mind being Jesi's guinea pig to help her properly use and control her powers. Maggie said she enjoyed teaching her the craft. Maggie knew all the spells and potions. Even without an active power, anyone could cast a spell as long as they did it right. It just took longer. And you needed more herbs and crystals and an occasional rabbit's heart on hand to complete the spells. Jesi never asked where Maggie got the hearts from.

While Jesi learned at an advanced pace, she still felt behind and less knowledgeable than the other members of the coven. She didn't belong. Her mother felt the same way. They were just different. Jesi still didn't feel at one with her power. Getting a new backstory with every touch drained her. She didn't know if she was strong enough. Now, she had to go over her morning with Sylvia, which included Detective Charles Massey.

As Maggie talked on the phone, Jesi pulled out a blank piece of paper and began writing facts she knew about all three children, the two taken and Amber. As a corporate lawyer, she rarely had to work at lightning speed and she never felt connected to her clients. Things were different now. She knew those kids. She talked to them and watched them play. They were tiny humans taken from their family, from *her* family. There had to be a way to narrow down who took them and why.

She was still writing when Maggie handed the phone to Jesi. She wasn't ready. She pressed the phone to her ear and slowed her breathing.

"Hey, Sylvia." Maggie squeezed Jesi's arm and moved to give her privacy.

"Jesi," Sylvia said. "I understand you had a busy morning. Maggie has told me most of it, but I want to hear your version."

"You don't believe Maggie?" That surprised Jesi.

"Of course, I believe Maggie, but having a second set of eyes means that less is missed. You may have seen something she didn't. Or I may ask a question that Maggie didn't think to ask."

Jesi didn't know what to say to that. This was honestly her first time in the field, so to speak. Maggie did this stuff all the time. Gathering information, meeting with coven members, and researching. Researching was most of Jesi's experience with the coven. The last time they really wanted her help was with a legal issue two years ago. Now, there were missing children. The two situations proved quite different.

Maggie and she talked to Sylvia several times over the last week. All in person. This was the first phone conversation. Protocol wasn't something they wrote down. This wasn't the first time Jesi wanted it in writing.

"Where do you want me to start?" she asked.

"At Genevieve's house."

Jesi detailed what happened with Amber and what happened with the intruder. Jesi left nothing out except Chuck.

"And then we came here," Jesi said. "Maggie's going to process the dust and she just handed me a bunch of books to go through."

"So, tell me why the detective was there?" Sylvia asked.

"Maggie told you?" It shocked Jesi to think that Maggie told Sylvia about Detective Massey.

"No. Judy mentioned it," Sylvia said.

"Oh." While she was grateful Maggie also skipped over the detective, Jesi hoped she would have more time to process him before she talked to the coven leader. "Well," Jesi began, "I went to the police station hoping to glean some information from the detective in charge of the first two kidnappings. And I met Detective Charles Massey."

"And he went with you to Genevieve's house because?" Sylvia enunciated each word.

"He was at the shop when Judy called." Jesi tried to sound casual.

"Do I need to ask a question for every answer I need, or do you just want to tell me what you are hiding?"

"I can't glean anything from the detective." Jesi spoke as fast as she could.

There was silence from Sylvia's end of the phone. Jesi could hear her heart beating. She didn't know why she was so nervous. The Coven leader couldn't stop the connection with Chuck.

"Hello?" Jesi asked into the phone. Did Sylvia hang up?

"Do you know what that means?" Sylvia's voice was soft.

"He's my complement." Jesi stilled. She hadn't admitted it out loud. The heavy feeling lifted. Admission was the first step to solving a problem. Or something. Chuck wasn't exactly a problem until he started arresting people for magic.

"A law officer complement." Sylvia paused.

Jesi heard Sylvia's nails drum on the table on the other end of the line. She could almost hear her thinking.

"This could be interesting. When can I meet him?" Sylvia asked.

"Meet him?" Was she kidding? Jesi wasn't sure if she wanted to see him again.

"Yes. Meet him. He will be part of the family."

"I'm not marrying him," Jesi said.

"But he will be like a best friend," Sylvia said. Maggie told her the same thing. "The yin to your yang."

"The yin to my yang?" Jesi asked.

"You should tell her you want to be the yin," Maggie called across the room. So much for privacy.

"Your Gigi was always happiest when she was with your Grandpa," Sylvia said. Her tone softened. "Give this detective a chance. And I want to meet him as soon as possible."

"Um… I'll see what I can do."

"We'll touch base soon. Bye, Jessica."

Jesi hung up the phone. She didn't know what to expect from Sylvia regarding Chuck, but that wasn't it. How was she supposed to approach him? 'Hey, Detective, wanna meet my aunt? She's the High Witch and if you are nice, she won't turn you into a opossum.'

"Shit," Jesi cussed under her breath. She looked up and Maggie was already beside her.

"What'd she say?" Maggie's eyes were wide and curious. She was so nosy, but Jesi loved her anyway. She would carry any secret to the grave.

"She called me Jessica at the end of the conversation."

"Shit!"

"And she wants to meet Chuck."

"Double shit. Ol' Chuckers is screwed."

"Yeah. Especially since I'm not sure I want to see him again."

"Really?" Maggie sounded surprised. Her eyes softened as she put an arm over Jesi's shoulder.

"If you don't want to see him again, I will respect that decision," Maggie said, "and stand with you when you tell Aunt S because you know she won't forget. But I really want you to think about it. He could be a great friend. Something in the world thinks you two have a connection. It might be worth finding out what that connection is."

Maggie hugged Jesi and then placed a book in front

of her. Companions, Complements, and Magic. Jesi looked down at the book and then at the notes she wrote about the children before the talk with Sylvia. She picked up the paper. There was a pattern.

"Maggie," Jesi started. "I have an idea about the kidnappings." Jesi handed Maggie her notes on the children. "Amber can burn things, Pattie can create mist, and Aiden can move air. I think he's looking for elemental witches. Children are easier to grab and control. Whatever spell he's using needs the four elements."

Maggie stared at Jesi's notes. "Son of a bitch," she said. "You're a genius. That gives us time. He's dead in the water without fire and earth. And we know for a fact he doesn't have fire."

"We need to call Sylvia back and put extra protection on anyone who can manipulate any type of fire or earth," Jesi said.

"Not it!" both girls said.

Jesi pointed and laughed at Maggie. "I said it first," she sang at Maggie.

"Fine," Maggie said with a heavy sigh as she picked up her phone.

~

The shop was slow, but Maggie and Jesi stayed busy. The witch line kept Maggie tied up for most of the day. She coordinated the information gathered from various members of the coven, specifically the watchers. The coven members who lived on the outskirts of the area are called watchers. They monitored anything moving through the region.

While Maggie and Jesi weren't the only ones researching the kid's disappearance, the process was still slow. Too slow for Jesi. She closed the book she was looking through when Maggie called her back to the workshop.

The work bench looked pristine, with candles on each of the corners. Maggie closed the door behind Jesi when she walked inside. Jesi slowed down her stride and studied Maggie. That door never closed. Jesi looked back at it and touched it. The door was still solid.

"Stop being weird," Maggie said. She moved books and papers to the other workbench and came back with her notebook. She handed it to Jesi and physically grabbed her by the arm and moved her in front of the workbench.

"You could use your words," Jesi said.

Her head followed Maggie as she continued about the room. Maggie finally moved beside Jesi and handed her a small vial. It was the vial with the black substance from Amber's room.

"Look over the spell in your hand." Maggie rubbed her hands on the sides of her pants.

Jesi looked down at the notebook. The layout of the table was identical to a drawing on the pad. Beside the drawing was the spell. Jesi read over it and looked at Maggie, eyebrows furled. Over the last year, Maggie asked Jesi to do certain spells that would take her much longer to perform, since she doesn't have a power.

"So, we pour the contents in the middle of the table, I say this spell while holding a rock." Jesi looked at the notebook again. "Yes, a rock. And then something will happen. That's what it says 'Holding a rock' and 'something will happen'."

"Yes," Maggie said with a glare. "You will hold this rock, and something will happen." She took the notebook out of Jesi's hand and replaced it with a small dark blue stone.

"Is this sodalite?" Jesi asked. She looked up with a raised eyebrow.

"It should help you focus and garner knowledge for the spell to work."

"Do you know what's going to happen when I say the spell?" Jesi asked with her hands on her hips.

"Sort of," Maggie said. "Here, empty the vial in the center of the table, then hold the sodalite over the material and read the spell. I'll hold the notebook for you and then record everything that happens. The spell should hold anywhere from ten to thirty minutes." She stood and held the book out for Jesi to read.

"You couldn't have given me this earlier to prepare?" Jesi huffed out.

"What's to prepare?" Maggie asked.

"Mentally prepare." Jesi shook herself, poured the vial onto the table, and held the rock over it. She began the spell.

"Used up spell bits
Left Behind
Feel my magic

So defined

Single out and separate

Classify what made it create."

As she spoke, power flowed through her. It pushed up through her feet and down from her head, all rushing toward her outreached hand. Her eyes stayed glued to the smudge of dirt in the middle of the table. The pressure built around her hand, but it wouldn't release. Nothing else was written on the paper, so she willed the power to leave her.

Maggie said something, but the force of the spell echoed in her ears, drowning out Maggie's voice. She glanced at Maggie to see her mouthing something and waving her arms about.

Jesi took in a sharp breath, the light turning on as she turned toward the table and said, "So mote it be."

The power cascaded out of her rock clutched hand on to the black smudge and reflected multicolored light. With a flash, the tabletop glowed white and dimmed to reveal small drawings on the table. Each appeared etched with light and were small diagrams of leaves and herbs and flowers and tiny insects. Jesi dropped her arm as Maggie began writing everything she saw into the notebook. Jesi took out her phone and snapped pictures with the hope they would show up later.

"Remember," Maggie said, "let the magic flow through you. The big spells need the ending words like 'so mote it be' to close the spell."

"I should have remembered that," Jesi said with a sigh. "How long will this last again?"

"About twenty-five minutes for Gigi. So, maybe fifteen minutes on average? It holds longer the more powerful the witch. I want to get as much information down in case it fades before then." Maggie continued to copy the drawings and identify them in her notebook.

"Where did you find this spell?" Jesi asked.

"In the margins of one of Gigi's notebooks. It's much simpler than the one I've used before."

"It's perfect," Jesi said, staring at the drawings.

This could be a tremendous breakthrough for the case. They could narrow down suspects based on the spell ingredient list. She identified at least one ingredient that was scarce and likely bought at Maggie's shop. The more she stared at the table, the more she felt she was missing something. Just at the tip of her tongue. Something that would put this all together.

She looked at her watch. It was getting late, and she was feeling the stress from the long day. She rolled her shoulders and felt the stiffness. Maggie sighed. Jesi glanced at her and could see the bags under her eyes. The light faded from the table.

"It was short-lived," Jesi said. "Only fifteen minutes."

"Well, Gigi packed a punch when it came to casting spells. You'll get there." Maggie rubbed one of Jesi's shoulder and blew out the candles and, with Jesi's help, cleaned up the table.

Jesi couldn't stop glancing over at Maggie. She moved slower than usual, and she drummed her fingers enough today to put grooves in the counter. Jesi packed up her bags and headed toward the door, but turned around, walked back to Maggie, and gave her a hug.

"What's that for?" Maggie asked.

"You're working hard," Jesi said. "Go home. Rest. We won't find anyone if we are too tired to think."

"I'm not that tired."

"The bags under your eyes tell me differently," Jesi said. "Now, go home and sleep. Send Sylvia an update and let them research tonight."

"You're not the boss of me," Maggie grumbled with a smile.

"Don't make me call my mom," Jesi said with a wink as they both walked out and locked up the store. Tonight would be for sleep.

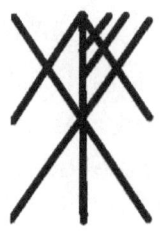

Chapter 7

After a fitful night of dreams filled with a certain handsome detective, Jesi parked across the street from the magic shop. With limited parking in this part of Savannah, they parked on the street and were lucky it was without meters.

She climbed out of her car and turned to see Chuck walking towards her. Air caught in her chest as she watched him stride. His confidence was evident with every step, and even though he wore slacks and a jacket as a detective, she wanted to see how handsome he would be in a uniform. She swallowed hard and let out the breath she was holding as he stopped in front of her.

"Miss Osman," he said, offering his arm. "May I walk you to the store?"

His smile made her forget about her fitful night of sleep. She put her hand through his elbow, and they crossed the street.

"What brings you by this early in the morning?" Jesi

asked.

"I have a few more questions, if you have the time," he said.

"I'll check my calendar when we get in the shop." Jesi stopped in front of the door and let go of his elbow. She dug in her bag for the keys and smiled at him. She felt like a fool, but she missed looking into his eyes, which was the cornerstone of her dreams last night. With key in hand, she turned to the door and froze. What an idiot. She gave too much attention to Chuck; she didn't even see the door was ajar. The lights were still off, so she knew Maggie wasn't there yet.

"Oh no," was all she said. Who would break into the magic shop and how did Maggie not know?

"Did you leave the door open last night?" Chuck asked.

Jesi turned to see him standing with his gun in his hands, ready to investigate.

"No," she said, "I distinctly remember locking the door last night."

Chuck nodded. "Wait here," he said and pushed the door open with his foot disappearing inside.

From the door, she saw some racks on the floor and merchandise scattered. She turned to look for Maggie while she reached for her phone, and saw Maggie's car pull into a parking spot behind hers. Maggie sat in her car and stared at Jesi. Her eyebrows bunched together. Jesi could see her ask 'what?' from across the street. Jesi waved her over. Maggie got out of the car and made her way across the street.

"What are you doing standing outside with the door open?" Maggie asked.

"The door was open when I got here," Jesi said. "Chuck is inside now, I guess clearing the place."

Maggie stared at Jesi with her mouth open. She looked back and forth from Jesi to the shop. "What?" She asked. "Why... I don't understand."

"I don't either," Jesi said as she pulled Maggie into a hug.

Jesi let the recent memories from Maggie wash over her. Maggie was often Jesi's guinea pig when she practiced her power and knew what to expect from her. And some people were worth the discomfort.

"How am I... How long will we... Do you think insurance will cover this?" Maggie asked.

"Yes, insurance will cover this," Jesi said and grabbed Maggie's upper arms. "Insurance will cover this. You call them. Do you want me to call Sylvia?"

"No. I'll call her after." Maggie stared blankly at the shop. "Do you think they took anything besides money? We don't have a lot of cash on site, anyway."

"We will know more when Chuck comes out," Jesi said. She rubbed Maggie's arms.

"Will we be able to open today?" Maggie's voice was soft and small. Jesi didn't know Maggie could sound so lost.

"I don't know. Do you think you'll want to open today?"

"I don't know," Maggie said. Her voice sounded hollow. She looked at Jesi, "What would Gigi do?"

Jesi looked into Maggie's eyes, the eyes of a little kid looked up to her. It was a look that she never received from anyone from the coven, much less Maggie. Maggie, who studied the craft harder than anyone. Maggie, who learned everything she knew from the previous Coven leader. Maggie, who should be the next coven leader, asked her for advice.

"She would demand to know answers," Jesi said, "and that's what we are going to do now. She would take care of business. Do you know what you would do?"

Maggie shook her head.

"You would make a list and get it done," Jesi said. "First, call the insurance company. Second, we will get a police report from Chuck. While we wait, we will call Sylvia and then reinforcements to help us clean. And when the shop opens back up, we are going to clean it."

"You're right," Maggie said, squaring her shoulders. "This is not the time to go to pieces. It's just a shop."

Jesi smiled at Maggie and they both turned to look at the darkened building. When Chuck exited the building, Jesi heard Maggie whisper, "And it's just my livelihood."

~

Chuck left the shop after he called it into the station and saw Jesi and Maggie. They looked at him, wanting answers. Jesi rubbed Maggie's back as she gave him a half smile. Maggie's face was pale with dark circles under her eyes. Her lips were in a tight, thin line. No smile or frown. It was a stark difference from how animated she was yesterday.

"How bad is it?" Maggie asked.

The force of her gaze surprised him. "They ransacked everything," he said. "It's hard to tell if they took anything. I'll need you to do an inventory once the scene is clear. Also, there is a door in the workshop area that I can't open."

"The library," Maggie said. She closed her eyes and sighed. "You won't be able to open it without the key."

"I need to do a sweep," he said. "Do you have the key on you?"

"Do you think he could even get in?" Jesi asked Maggie. "He shouldn't even see the door."

"I know," Maggie snapped and shrugged away from Jesi. She reached into her pocket, produced a key, and held it out to Chuck. "When you put the key in the lock, say 'hunker bubble' and turn the key. If it doesn't turn, it doesn't turn."

Chuck squeezed Maggie's arm and took the key. "Backup will be here shortly. I'll be right back after I've cleared the library."

Chuck made sure Maggie nodded her head before he went back into the shop. He stepped over fallen displays and moved into the workshop area with the locked door. The workshop still had bundles of herbs hanging along the walls despite the amount of debris scattered across the floor.

He put the key into the door and said, "hunker bubble." He imagined what he looked like to an observer. Ridiculous. He felt ridiculous. Who came up with the phrase 'hunker bubble'? Chuck turned the key and pushed on the door. It didn't budge. He wiggled the key and the doorknob. It was the same as before, but the door was now presumably unlocked. He took the key out and made his way back to Jesi and Maggie.

Once outside, he saw Maggie writing in a notebook and Jesi looked over her shoulder. He walked over to the pair and handed Maggie the key. "The door still wouldn't open." Maggie nodded and put the key back in her pocket.

"Does that mean that when the wards fell, the backup ward on the library went into effect?" Jesi asked.

"See," Maggie said, "you are learning."

"Wards?" Chuck asked as he watched the two ladies.

Maggie stared at the shop as Jesi took the notebook from her and wrote in it herself.

"A ward is a magical barrier, generally placed around a static location like a home or store," Jesi said. "We put a ward on the shop each night. If someone passes over it, Maggie will get a wake-up call. She didn't get the call, which means the person who did this broke the wards with magic."

"How did that..." Chuck said, "uh, backup ward activate?"

"It's a little complicated," Jesi said.

She seemed more comfortable and confident today. Her hair was down. The natural curls framed her face, making her appear less stern. The curls made her hair look too short to put into a ponytail at all. He squashed the urge to touch it and to touch her.

"When we leave," she continued, "we put up the ward. When we come back, we unlock the ward. If you break the ward, it has consequences. Like with a safe, if you use the code, you can use the safe over and over. But if you break the safe, it no longer works. The ward around the library is much more powerful than that on the store. When the store wards fall without the proper incantation, it activates the library wards, making it impossible to enter from this side of the room. We will have to rebuild the wards. Or Maggie will."

Maggie walked away during Jesi's explanation and sat on the curb. Chuck's backup arrived.

"I'm going to go talk to the team. I'll come back to get statements from both of you shortly. Don't go anywhere," Chuck said.

Jesi nodded. Chuck gave her a small smile and went to talk to the uniformed officers.

~

Jesi sat down beside Maggie on the curb. "I still can't believe you gave him the key and code word."

"I can't believe he could even see the door." Maggie picked up a small pebble off the ground and skidded it on the road.

"What do you mean?"

"Part of the powerful ward going into effect glamours the door to outsiders," Maggie said. "The connection between you two is growing. I should tell Em."

"No, you shouldn't." Jesi sighed. "It feels fast. Too fast and I'm not ready. Plus, I, well, we have more important things to deal with."

"So, you're not ready to have a best friend for life?" Maggie asked, her eyes still on the road. She threw another pebble. "Anyway, I would say this is an escalation, except it's not. Breaking and entering is less concerning than kidnapping, though I wonder what he was looking for."

Jesi turned to watch the officers go in and out of the shop. "If we find out who did this, do you want to sue them?" Jesi asked. "I know an excellent lawyer."

"No. I want to punch them in the face," Maggie said and threw another pebble harder. "Do you think they will let us in sometime soon?"

"They will if you tell them about the security system."

"I'll tell Chuckers, but I don't trust the others."

"You met Chuck yesterday. How can you trust him more than the others?"

"Well, he is your best friend," Maggie said before she stood up and dusted herself off.

Jesi followed suit, just in time to see Chuck walk over to them.

"So, this should take a few hours. I also have a few questions," Chuck said and pulled out his notebook from the inside of this jacket pocket.

"We will answer any questions you have. But can you talk to Jesi first?" Maggie smiled at Jesi. "I have to call my insurance company. When do you think I can get a police report?"

"In a few days, I'm sure," Chuck said.

"Great. Just let Jesi know when it's available." Maggie turned, walked away, and pulled out her phone.

"So, can you tell me about the security of the shop?" Chuck was in full detective mode. He held his pen and notebook, ready to write.

"You know about the magic wards, which you can't write about. The door has a bolt, and the windows are all locked from the inside before we leave," Jesi said. "And… there is a security system, only it's a magical system. Or it's hidden magically. It's not something that we can show to just anyone."

"What?" The deadpan look made Jesi squirm. This might be harder than she thought.

"Security system. It's a regular camera system hidden by magic. You know magic. Like me?" Jesi wide eyed him.

"How exactly does…" Chuck waved his hands around. "Um, well, just show me after the scene is clear?"

"Just so we are on the same page," Jesi said, "we are only showing you. How long will it take to clear the scene?"

"A few hours at most. We will take as much evidence as we can, and then with whatever the security system shows us, we can go from there," Chuck said. "And I'm not sure any other officers know about this, so yeah. Just me."

Jesi nodded and looked at the front of the store. A few officers congregated around outside the door. She looked up at Chuck when she felt his hand on her shoulder.

"You have nothing to worry about," he said. "If you want, we can post an officer here for the next few days."

"Oh. No, I think we will be okay."

"Just to be safe, I'll stop in to check on things." He squeezed her shoulder with a smile.

"You are taking this magic stuff well," Jesi said, and she meant it. When he left the day before, she thought she'd never see him again.

"I'm still processing. I'm not sure how much of it to believe," Chuck said. Jesi moved her hand to cover his on her shoulder.

"You need to believe it all." Jesi could look in his eyes all day and she wanted to feel the scruff of his face on hers.

"You two having a staring contest?" Maggie said as she walked up to them.

"Yes. It is part of the investigation," Chuck answered with a wink to Jesi.

"Nice." Maggie stood with her hands on her hips like she was ready for action. "Jesi will be the stand in for all contests."

Chuck's hand dropped from Jesi's shoulder. Maggie's eyebrow rose as she looked at Jesi.

"So, I talked to the insurance company. They will call the station to get the report in a few days and are sending someone out today to survey the damage. I also spoke with Aunt Sylvia. She will check on the status of the library ward from her end. And I will do the same once we get inside. The library holds the most valuable and rare items.

The rest, you know, just makes me money." Maggie frowned.

"Oh, Maggie." Jesi wrapped her arm around her. "I know you're worried. The shop will be up and running tomorrow. No worries."

"Alright," Maggie said and walked over to her car and sat on the hood.

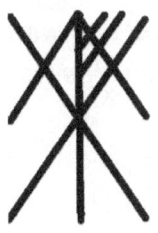

Chapter 8

Once Chuck finished taking their statement, the rest of the morning went by quickly as he and the team gathered what little evidence they could find. He wanted to be thorough. If this break-in had anything to do with the missing children, it could mean a break in the case.

After the police cleared the shop, Chuck followed the two women inside. Maggie led the way through the door and slowed down. She stepped through the wreckage and frowned as she tried to pick up racks off the floor. Chuck went over and helped her with a few.

She turned away from him and walked toward the back room with the hanging herbs and work benches. Jesi trailed after Maggie and looked back at Chuck. Jesi smiled at Chuck while they waded through the downed displays. He smiled back, despite his brain telling him to be professional.

They all walked into what Chuck thought of as a workspace. It was the least destroyed room in the place.

Herbs still hung above the window facing the street. Everything from the benches was on the floor, but they still stood upright.

Maggie and Jesi moved to the wall away from the window. Maggie turned to Jesi. "Do you want to?" Maggie asked. Jesi chewed her bottom lip.

"I don't think I remember the words," Jesi whispered.

Chuck pretended not to hear and looked toward the windows.

"Okay, Chuckers," Maggie said as she walked past Chuck. She pinched off bits of the herbs drying over the window and pulled the curtain shut before she walked back toward the back wall.

"So, magic lesson number one." Maggie smiled at Chuck. "I do not have an active power. Everything I do comes from a combination of ritual and word play or spell casting. Some spells are easier than others. Those with active powers have an easier time casting spells. They can forgo ritual and sometimes, the words."

Maggie rubbed the herbs between both hands. Chuck looked toward Jesi. She wrapped her arms around herself. Chuck wasn't sure what was about to happen. Jesi didn't look at him now. He wanted to put his arms around her and protect her from whatever Maggie was about to do.

Maggie smiled at both of them. "Are we ready?" Jesi nodded and took a step back toward Chuck. He nodded.

Maggie mumbled something under her breath. She stepped back and threw the herb mixture on the wall in an arc and said, "security." The word echoed in the room. The wall glowed a bright blue as the herbs fell, and previously unseen electronics protruded from it as if pushing through a slime. Everything stopped shimmering, and a table sat against the wall with the computers and monitors, all on and showing video.

"'Security'?" Chuck looked at Maggie. "That is your magic word?" She shrugged. Jesi had her head in her hand.

"There's more to it, but yeah. It's easy to remember." She pulled a chair from the corner of the room and sat down at one computer. "And very few people will try something so obvious."

Jesi pulled two chairs from the other room. Chuck took a seat beside Maggie with Jesi on his other side. "This looks like a normal set up," he said.

"Oh, it is," Jesi said. "It is just magically hidden, so people don't know they are being recorded and they don't mess with the tapes."

"It was actually Jesi's idea." Chuck smiled at Jesi while Maggie spoke. "Our Gigi had this system and worried people would mess with it. Jesi said she should hide it. Gigi asked, 'Well where?' All huffy like she would get. Jesi looked at her and said, 'With magic'," Maggie laughed. Jesi tried to cover her face. "Gigi's expression was so funny. I'll never forget it."

Both girls were smiling now. Some of the tension left the room.

"Anyway," Jesi said. "I think we should start after we left last night. What time was that? Around 8:15?"

"Yeah. Let me see." Maggie pulled the footage up. Chuck followed along. This scene wasn't as common as he would have liked. Most small shop owners didn't have the funds for a camera system.

"Stop." Chuck pointed to the screen. "What time is that? 1:12." Chuck wrote that down. He knew many people thought he was a little ridiculous with his notes, but it came in handy over the years. "Okay, let's watch the full video once with each camera."

They all sat in the small room staring at the figure that was tearing apart the place. No one spoke. Chuck could barely hear them breathe. After the last camera played, they all sat staring at the screens. Chuck didn't want to disturb them. He looked at Jesi and her face was pale. Maggie had tears streaming down her cheeks.

"So, we never got a good look at the intruder. His hood stayed up the entire time, and he kept his head down. All we have to go on is height. About 5' 10" I would say."

Chuck made sure the two ladies paid attention. Jesi nodded in agreement. Maggie's head had dropped.

"It's the same guy from Amber's house. He walks the same. Has on the same clothes," Jesi said.

"Now, he came to this room first. Is there something in here that anyone would want?"

They both looked around the room. "Drying herbs? Or the safe?" Maggie said. "But he didn't even touch the safe. And all these herbs are common. The special herbs are usually ordered and dried off site or kept in the magic room for purchase."

"This is your workbench," Jesi said. Her dark blue eyes stared at Maggie. Maggie looked confused.

"And?" Maggie asked.

"And you and I sat here last night going over the powder we took from Amber's bedroom."

"Do you really think he would come here to get it back?"

"Maybe," Jesi said, "if there is something about that powder that can link him to the crimes."

"Jesi's right." It impressed Chuck. Although, it shouldn't. She was a lawyer after all, but it was nice seeing her so confident. "Where is the sample now?"

"In my bag," Maggie said. She pointed to the bag on the floor beside her.

"Were you able to figure anything out?"

"I have the key ingredients list. I was going to spend most of today going through the books trying to link them all together."

"You should go through your sale receipts to see who bought all those items recently. When I get the analysis back from the lab, I can officially help you in that regard," Chuck said.

Jesi put a hand on Chuck's shoulder. A warmth seeped into him from her touch.

"I need to get a copy of this back to the lab. Our video analysis group might be able to get more out of it."

"Yeah. I'll download it now." Maggie turned back to the computer and pulled the footage.

"Thank you for being here today," Jesi said. "Why were you here this morning, anyway?"

"I came about the powder and to ask more questions about this magic."

"A little overwhelming, huh?" Jesi smiled at him. Chuck smiled back. He couldn't help it.

"Yeah. That's not the only thing."

~

After Chuck dropped off the security footage, he made his way over to his father's auto shop again. He walked through the small waiting room and straight to the back and knocked on his father's open door. Alan looked up.

"My son, the detective," he smiled and waved him into the room. "You remember Keon?"

"Yeah," Chuck said, "how are you doing?" They shook hands as Keon left the office.

"Two visits in one week," Alan said. "I must be doing something right or something wrong." His smile reached his eyes and accentuated his crow's feet.

"Well, I kinda met someone. And it's very complicated."

"How so? She already married?"

"No," Chuck said. "It's Jesi from the magic shop."

"Ah," said Alan. He stopped flipping through a parts catalog and looked at Chuck.

"She's the witch that turned the rock into a worm," said Chuck. "That I'm attracted to. Can I date a witch?"

"I don't see why not." Alan laughed. "I know of at least three wolves married to humans. I don't imagine it's that much different for witches." He paused with a frown.

"Your mother and I taught you that you should accept people for who they are. And if you want to be friends or date someone, that should be something decided by the people involved, not society." He came over to Chuck and slapped him on the back. "But, if you want, I can call Keon back in here. I think he's dating a witch. Or his sister is dating one. Either way, he could give you better advice than your old man."

"No, I think your advice is enough for me." Chuck smiled at his dad, then raised an eyebrow. His dad's eyes widened at the look.

"Does Mom know about magic?" Chuck asked.

Alan laughed. It was his deep belly laugh that the staff often heard out in the shop through the walls. "Yes, your mother knows. And I've told her you know. So maybe you can come by sometime with your crush and we can have dinner."

"Crush?" Chuck said. "What am I? Eight?"

Alan laughed his way out of the office.

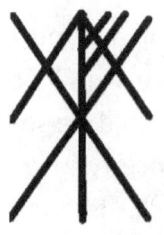

Chapter 9

Jesi slung her bag on the kitchen counter and kicked off her shoes. The small apartment she had was just what she needed. A place full of peace and quiet. It was the one place that wasn't completely filled with magic. After putting the shop back together, it was exactly where she wanted to be.

The only space here that she allowed any sort of magic was the kitchen. She used her kitchen to try any spells she didn't want Maggie to know about. Specifically, the one that could give her freedom. From her pocket, she pulled out a small vial filled with a black liquid. It smelled like cinnamon and licorice. She imagined it tasted like a shot of Fireball and Jager mixed together. Jesi hated both, preferring a nice dry red wine.

Shaking the vial, she watched the color fade to a dark gray. The potion only lasted around seven days, and for the last six months, she'd made that potion once a week. Each week proved how chicken shit she was. She would never take the potion; she just liked having the option.

But these last few days, the pull to down the drink was stronger than ever. She'd gleaned five times as many people in the last few days than the last year. It drained her and tested her sanity. Surely there was a way she could help those children without powers. Maggie did it every day. She stared at the fading potion. She memorized the recipe months ago, yet she pulled out the spell hidden in one of her kitchen drawers. The Power Stripping potion was designed to strip any witch's individual power for life.

The original book listed the reasons for the potion's use on the edges of the page. They all pointed to its use as a punishment for the highest crimes or a way to protect the coven. None of the reasons listed "I don't wanna" or "magic ruined my life".

Jesi opened the vial and poured its contents down the drain. She turned on the water and diluted the mixture. Tonight, she would brew another. She cleared a space and pulled ingredients, pots, and cutting boards out of the cabinets. She placed the pot on a burner and set to work making the potion. With all the ingredients prepped and her makeshift cauldron warm, she mixed all the ingredients and brought it to a boil. She turned it down to a simmer, set the timer, and washed her hands.

She looked up and stared in the door's direction when she heard a knock. Another tap, this one louder, pulled her from her spot. It was nearing 10 o'clock at night and she rarely had visitors that didn't call first. She looked through the peephole and her eyes grew big. He knocked again with her eye pressed against the door. Startled, she pulled it open.

"Detective," Jesi said, "what brings you to my door?"

The door opened just enough for her to see him through the crack. She was too tired to smooth over what she could only imagine was an incredulous look.

"I was hoping we could talk some more," Chuck said, "if you aren't busy. And it's Chuck, remember?" He smiled at her and took a step toward the door.

Jesi took the chance to soak up the appearance of him standing in her doorway. He wore jeans and a plain green t-shirt that fit snug over his shoulders. She had no idea he was so muscular under the jacket he wore.

Jesi surprised herself and opened the door. She stepped aside to let him inside. She watched him stroll through the hallway and stop at the end of the tiny foyer. She pushed past him and led him into the small living room. There was enough room for a couch, a TV, and an end table. The living area had an open floor plan, so the dining room sat six feet away and the kitchen was separated only by a counter and was designed to have bar seating. Only she didn't have the stools. She sat on the couch and he sat next to her. She looked in his light blue eyes and felt her shoulders relax.

"You have a nice place," Chuck said as he settled into the couch.

"Yeah," Jesi said, "I like it because it's small. When I worked at the law firm, I was rarely home, so having a small space meant I had less to clean. Now, it's my comfort zone." Jesi shuffled her feet on the floor and relaxed on the couch.

"How's the shop?" he asked.

"It's clean enough to open tomorrow." Jesi rubbed her hands on her pants. "Maggie's going to need to order supplies to replace what they destroyed. She's holding it together right now, but I'm worried about her. She takes on a great deal of burden for the coven, and now, her shop was ransacked."

"Coven, eh?" Chuck asked.

"I probably shouldn't have said that," Jesi said.

"My father already mentioned it," Chuck said with a smile.

"Your father?" Jesi raised her eyebrows. "You told your dad?"

"I might have freaked out after you turned the rock into a worm," Chuck said. "My dad is the only person I know that could help me think rationally about it."

"Who's your dad?" she asked.

"He's Alan Massey of Massey and Sons Auto Shop," Chuck said.

"You're Alan Massey's son?" Jesi asked. "I didn't realize. The entire coven goes to his shop. And he never told you about the supernatural before?"

"Apparently, he didn't think I'd handle it well," Chuck explained. "I have a tendency to view things as strictly good or evil."

"Oh," Jesi said. She never saw the world as good or evil. She'd never met anyone who didn't see the world in shades of gray.

"You said that Maggie doesn't have an active

power," Chuck said. "Why is she so involved with the coven?"

"Maggie has always had a strong interest in magic. She has the knack, so to speak. When the rest of us went out to play after lessons, she would stay and ask for more. When she didn't get an active power, it devastated her. She tried not to let it show, but we all could tell. Gigi, our grandmother, was disappointed as well. Maggie was the star student, the one with the most promise. Honestly, even without a power, she can perform better magic than most of us with one. She knows what herbs to use, what words to say, and if she needs crystals or candles or whatever else."

Jesi shook her head and studied her hands. These were the hands of a quitter, a spoiled brat who wanted to throw away fate. She looked up at Chuck and gave him a slight grin.

"I was delighted I didn't have a power. I wanted to do more with my life than magic. My mom wanted more for me as well. With a power, you kinda get stuck in the family. My mom planned on moving away before she met my dad. She got as far as the next town over. She told me he was worth staying for, even if she had to deal with the coven."

"So, you got your power late?"

"Yes. Witches typically manifest an active power before puberty, if they will have one at all. I developed mine a year ago, when Gigi died. Her power transferred to me. Everyone was shocked, none more than me."

"What about your mom? What's her power?"

"She can smell emotions. She hates it, but it was kinda useful for raising me."

"That's… not what I expected. I thought witches made potions or turned people into toads." He wiggled his fingers in the air like a stage magician.

"Oh, some can do amazing things. My cousin, Vera, can track people down with only a picture, but she's working in England, and we can't get in touch with her. Sylvia, my aunt, can levitate things. She usually only moves small things, but Maggie told me she's been training on larger objects since she became the head of the coven."

"So, she wants to do the heavy lifting figuratively and literally?"

Jesi laughed. "Yes. She is stepping up to the plate." Her laughter died down and she could hear the crickets outside chirp.

"So, why did you go into law?" Chuck asked.

"I've always wanted to help people," Jesi said. "And I love being right." She laughed.

"And so, you chose corporate law?"

"It's where I could get a job and it paid well. It's also exciting. I loved figuring out how to win."

She sat back and studied Chuck. His calm demeanor washed over her. His elbows rested on his knees, leaning toward her as he listened. She rarely had anyone listen to her with such intent. "After years in law school, sometimes you forget what path you want to go down and are just grateful you got a job so you can pay your student loans."

"I can understand that," Chuck said.

"So, Detective," Jesi said, "why did you become a cop?"

"I have always wanted to be a cop," Chuck said. "Like yourself, I want to help people in a more tangible sense. I always thought cops were brave and noble, and that is what I wanted to be."

"Brave and noble Chuck," Jesi smiled. "So, you wanted to be a knight that solved cases."

"Yes. I wanted to be Sherlock Holmes with a gun and the law behind me," he said. "Doesn't the coven help people, too?"

"They do, only I never saw that side of it before," Jesi sighed. "It looked like a group of people who did magic together. Nothing ever really happened. The last six months working with Maggie has shown me how much the coven looks out for the members and the supernatural community as a whole."

"Just the last six months?"

"We've had some weird events happen lately. But nothing like what's happening now." Jesi cocked her head to the side and watched Chuck. He rubbed his chin and nodded his head. "Have you dug up anything about the kid's disappearances?"

"No. The analysis of the substance nor the recording has come back from the lab. We should know more tomorrow."

"We were able to pull some information from our sample. We plan on starting fresh tomorrow, going over sales for the last six months. Maggie's probably already started." Chuck was smiling at Jesi as she spoke. Jesi gave in and grinned.

"What did you find in your sample?" Chuck asked.

"Just a long list of herbs. I didn't think to send you a copy. I'm sorry. Come by tomorrow and we can get it for you."

He looked away. When he turned back, his smile vanished and said, "You said you would explain something to me. I think it's time."

"What am I going to explain to you?" Jesi asked.

"Why can't you use your power on me?"

Jesi braced herself. "That might take a while," she said.

"I have awhile to listen," Chuck said, leaning back.

Jesi sucked in a deep breath and let it out slowly. She broke away from his penetrative stare and focused on the floor. She didn't know if she was ready. But Jesi was strong. She dug deep down within herself and pulled up the confidence that made her a brilliant lawyer. She looked back at Chuck and spoke in a slow, even voice.

"Every witch with an active power has a complement. A complement is one person who suits that witch perfectly, so perfectly that the witch's innate power has no effect on that person. After consulting books, papers, journals, etc, we are pretty sure you are my complement."

"What?" Chuck raised his right eyebrow.

"Maggie says it's like finding your best friend," Jesi said. "We complement each other. We are fully compatible."

"Like a soul mate?" Chuck asked.

His eyebrows scrunched together. That kind of scrutiny from people didn't bother Jesi, but for some reason, her hands felt sweaty.

"Some people think of it that way, but I don't think it's the same sort of soul mate pull that werewolves have," Jesi said. She stopped herself short of a full ramble.

"Werewolves have soul mates?" Chuck asked.

"Yeah. It's a smell thing," Jesi said. She made herself keep her lips shut.

"What?" Chuck said. "You know what, we can go over that later. So, if your power doesn't work on me, so I'm automatically your complement?"

"No," Jesi replied, grateful to be off the werewolf tangent. That would take even longer to cover. "There are other signs as well. Like when we touch, that shock that shoots through us. Through me. Do you feel it too?"

"Yes," Chuck said, scooting closer. "Like static shock, only I don't want to let go."

"Exactly," Jesi said. "And how I feel safe around you. I want to trust you, even though my head is telling me not to trust my gut."

"And how I want to touch you again just to feel the spark," Chuck said. "It's the warmth that pulls me in."

"Maggie says that not everyone feels the static thing. And you aren't a demon or witch that's manipulating any of this. She made sure of that when you came to the shop two days ago."

"I don't remember that," Chuck said. "How does that work?"

"The potpourri in your hand," Jesi reminded him.

"Yes. I remember. It was very peculiar."

"You'll get used to her. She can't stop the peculiar." Jesi laughed and slid closer so their knees almost touched.

"And all witches have a complement?" he asked.

"Yes," she answered, "but it is rare to find one. The only other people I knew who had a complement were Gigi and Gramps, and I just found that out two days ago."

"Would you call yourself lucky?" he asked. He smiled and picked up her hand.

"I haven't decided yet," she said.

The soothing static of his touch traced up her arm. The more they touched, the further up she could feel the sensation. He rubbed her hand with his thumb. Her breathing began to shallow and quicken in her chest as his blue eyes drew her closer.

This close, she could smell his cologne, or maybe it was his natural scent. The sandalwood she recognized, and it mixed with another aroma she couldn't identify. The sensation of his lips on hers ended that thought.

The warmth, tingle, and electric shock she felt with this kiss spread to every fiber of her body. She grasped the hand she was holding, reaching up with the other to caress his face. His other hand found its way onto the back of her neck. Each one pushed into the kiss, abandoning each other's hands to pull the other closer. Jesi's chest pressed against Chuck's hard muscles. She took the chance and licked his lips when a blaring beep startled the pair apart.

Chuck breathed fast and looked around the room. "What is that?" he asked.

"The potion."

Jesi jumped up and ran to the kitchen. This was the last place she wanted to be seeing how hot she was from that kiss. She wanted to be back on the couch, out of the warm kitchen, back in his arms. She pulled the pot from the hot eye and turned it off in the process. The potion needed to cool down, but that barely registered as she considered the extent of her beating heart from one chaste kiss.

She turned and looked at Chuck. He held the potion recipe she didn't put away before she answered the door.

~

Chuck read the title of the spell for a second time. Power Stripping. What exactly was Jesi doing? Was this something she planned to use on someone else, like the kidnapper, or on herself? She told him she wanted to go back to being a lawyer, but did she want it bad enough to take her own powers away? He watched Jesi clean up the counters and wipe away the mess. She refused to look at him.

"Jesi?" he asked. "What is this for?"

She brushed off nothing from the front of her shirt. "Oh, it's just a potion I needed to make."

"Power stripping," Chuck read. "This is a power stripping potion? Does it strip away the ability to do any magic or just your active power? Special power?"

"Active power," she said. She still refused to meet his eyes. "Yes, it strips away your active power. It's not important why I need this potion. It's just something I have to do." She snatched the paper out of Chucks hand and stuffed it into a drawer. She leaned against the counter and crossed her arms.

He stalked over to her and tried to get her to meet his eyes. "You were going to take this potion," he said, "weren't you? You want to take away your active power."

"It's really none of your business," she said. She turned her head away from him.

"Of course, it's my business," he said. He put his hand on her cheek and turned it toward him.

"No, it's not." Jesi shrugged him off. "What I do with my power is none of your concern. You want to find the kidnapper, and want to use my ability to find him faster."

"Yes, you're right," he said. "And you implied you would help me. How can you help if you can't do magic?"

"Is that all I am to you? Magic girl?" Jesi faced him at last. Her face was flushed and her eyes on fire. "If that's what you want, go talk to Maggie."

"I don't want to talk to Maggie," Chuck said. He wrapped his hands around her shoulders and resisted the urge to shake her. "I want to talk to you. Of course, I don't want you to be magic girl. I'm just, I'm surprised you would be willing to give up something that helps people."

"At what cost?" she asked. Her voice grew louder. "My sanity is slipping away every time I touch someone. I could be the key to catching the person putting those kids in danger, but I have to touch the right person."

"It's the same with being a cop," he said. "I could be one interview away from finding those kids, one clue, one phone call, one mistake, and that person will be in my grasp. Everyone goes through this feeling. You are not hopeless."

"I've never known stress like this." She shuddered in his hands. "Being a lawyer was much easier."

"When you helped yourself instead of others?" he asked.

"I helped others." Her eyes stayed sharp on him.

"You helped corporations and you know it. I looked up that law firm. They are practically as corrupt as the companies they represent. And that's what you want to go back to?" Chuck maintained eye contact. He wanted to yield and hold her close, but he knew he needed to push just a little more.

"No. I don't want to go back there," she yelled. "But I like having the option." She looked at her feet, her head hung low. She spoke softly and said, "I want the option to be normal again."

"I hate to break it to you, but no one is normal," he said. "Especially not lawyers."

She laughed. The sound reverberated around the small kitchen as he sighed with relief. When her laughter died down, he wrapped her in his arms. He held her close in a soft sway, soaked in her warmth.

"Don't take the potion," he murmured in her ear. "I don't understand all of this and I still have doubts, but the more I learn, the more I see what you have is a gift. You are fortunate. You can give a voice to people who might not otherwise have one."

He felt her rub her face into his chest. "I never thought of it that way. I only saw it as a way to stop someone, not lift them up."

"You should," he said. "I think you can do some good in the world, even if it's just in the weird world of magic."

"You still want to have a word for all of this," she said with a laugh.

"I do," He said. He kissed the top of her head. "I could say world of the weird. Or land of frou frou."

"You're going to get kicked out. Those names are terrible."

"The last time I believed in anything magical was when I was 7 and Jim Smith told me there was no Santa Claus."

"Jim's a jerk."

He felt her smile into his chest. He wasn't sure what the future held, but the connection he felt with Jesi grew stronger.

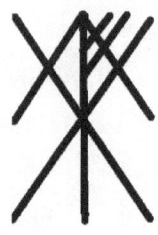

Chapter 10

Chuck walked into the station whistling. The night before went better than he hoped. The connection he felt with Jesi was unreal. He'd longed to find someone who understood the desire to help others.

Two days ago, she surprised him by walking into this station. Her confidence, which called him over to her, faltered with his touch. He thought about last night and had to stop himself from grinning like an idiot. He wasn't so sure he could. Holding her hand as she talked grounded him. Her dark blue eyes held knowledge and curiosity. He wanted to know everything that was behind those eyes.

Chuck sat down just as his phone rang. He answered the phone as he logged onto his computer. He was interested to see if the lab expedited his request or not.

"Detective Massey, this is Detective Sellers here in Macon."

"To what do I owe the pleasure, Detective?" Chuck

asked.

"A lab report was brought to my attention early this morning," Sellers said. "It seems like you found the same substance at a crime scene that I found here in Macon."

"I'm pulling up that report now. Tell me about your incident."

"A young child was kidnapped here nearly a week ago. We found a black substance at the crime scene, which is the same substance you found. Can I assume that you found this at a kidnapping as well?"

"An attempted kidnapping," Chuck said as he sat straight up in his chair. "We've had two kidnappings this past week and this would have been a third. The attempted kidnapping is unfortunately off the books for now. Can you send me your report on the missing child? I'll send you the reports we have and a write up on the attempted kidnapping ASAP."

"I'll send over what I have. I would like to offer my assistance in helping find the missing children," Sellers said.

"I'll talk to my supervisor about it and have a formal request sent over. I'll talk to you then," Chuck said.

"Thanks, Detective."

"No problem," Chuck said.

After they exchanged information, Chuck took a deep breath and gathered the details on the missing children. If this guy struck in Macon and then in Savannah, he could have moved on to another city by now. While he waited on the report from Detective Sellers, he printed off the lab report on the black substance. He would get to see Jesi sooner than he expected.

~

Jesi combed through the sales records at the shop. The handwriting was a little hard to read. The shop could use an upgraded system. She wondered if Maggie would go for it.

"Ugh, why are you smiling so much?" Emma asked.

Maggie recruited her to help look through the handwritten records. Being friends with Maggie so long meant Emma could read the chicken scratch.

"You are in a good mood today," Maggie said. "After they trashed this shop, you have the audacity to be happy."

She was pouring over books, looking for spells that matched the herbs. They could use an extra person. Sylvia was working on her end, but it didn't feel like it.

"No reason," Jesi said, but she couldn't stop herself from smiling.

Before Chuck left last night, he asked her out. She had a date with Chuck. It was a delightful feeling. He was handsome and had a big heart. His hands in hers felt like Heaven. She could touch again. And she wanted to touch every bit of that man. Maybe she just missed human companionship or just sex in general. Either way, she would not pass up this opportunity. And he had a nice ass.

"There, your smile got bigger," Maggie said, pointing. The book dropped to the floor as she leaned forward in her chair. "What's going on? You've been in a foul mood for a year. What changed?"

"Detective Massey is what changed," Emma said in a sing-song voice.

"Did you see him again yesterday?" Maggie asked.

"Maybe." Jesi felt her cheeks burn and tried to hide her face.

"Look at that blush." Emma reached out and pinched Jesi's cheeks.

"Stop." Jesi pushed her hand away and frowned.

"Tell us everything." Maggie propped her head in her hands. She looked like a little kid waiting for a bedtime story.

Jesi rolled her eyes and looked back at the receipts.

"Please," both girls said at the same time.

"Fine," Jesi said. "He came by my place last night to talk."

"Ooh," both girls said.

"Keep talking, mama," Maggie said.

"What did you talk about?" Emma used her hands to put quotes around the word talk.

"Really?" Jesi rolled her eyes. "Anyway... he asked me out. So, maybe I will give him a chance."

"Ooh," they said again.

"Giving him a chance in your pants," Emma said. Both girls high fived and giggled.

"Thanks," Jesi said. "I need new friends." She kept her smile to herself. She saw no need to encourage that behavior. Maggie would take it too far if Jesi showed approval.

"Oh, Jesi," Maggie said. "You know we love you. I'm thrilled for you. And if he isn't good to you, I'm learning all kinds of good spells I can use on him."

"Like what?" Emma asked. Emma and Maggie had always egged each other on.

"Two words," Maggie said. "Turtle penis."

Jesi couldn't help it. She laughed with them. They were laughing so hard, they didn't hear the bell from the door.

"Ladies, did I miss something?" Chuck stood at the counter looking over at them.

The laughter stopped, only to start again. Maggie fell out of her seat. Emma was pointing at her and Jesi tried to stop the laughter and covered her face. Chuck would just have to wait.

The laughter died down after Maggie ran to the back room and Emma fanned herself. Jesi looked up at Chuck as he raised an eyebrow to her and Emma when they stifled their giggles. Maggie came back out of the back room and handed everyone water.

"So, what brings you to our store so early?" Maggie asked.

Chuck looked around the shop. He smiled at Jesi each time he looked at her.

"The place looks nice. Y'all did a great job cleaning up."

"Thanks," Maggie said.

"We were here until about 8 last night. But you knew that already, didn't you?" Emma said.

She winked at Chuck. Jesi scowled at her.

"Is that a problem, Emma?" Chuck smiled back at Emma.

"I like him," Emma said to Maggie as she leaned back in her seat.

"Did you come here to check on the shop or for something else?" Jesi said. She held his stare with a smirk.

"I just got a call from a detective from Macon." Jesi felt her face fall. Frozen with wide eyes. Chuck's eyes didn't leave hers.

"A child was kidnapped from the Macon area almost a week ago," Chuck explained. "The same substance we found in Amber's room was also found in the child's room."

"What?" Jesi stood up. She looked over at Maggie. Her face was emotionless.

"What's the kid's name?" Maggie asked. She grabbed her bag and rummaged inside.

"The child's name is William Shaw," Chuck said.

Maggie pulled out a small book and flipped through the pages and picked up the old phone against the wall behind the counter. The witch line. Gigi upgraded the phone once when she realized that a rotary phone wasn't the best option anymore. She somehow kept the old ringtone.

"Hi, this is Margaret Watkins. I'm with the Moonlight Oak Coven here in Savannah."

Jesi watched Maggie. Maggie tapped her finger on the counter. Emma sat forward in her chair, elbows on her knees. She looked ready to bound out of her chair at any moment. Jesi grabbed a pen and paper and started writing frantically. "What time was he taken?" and "Do they have extra evidence?"

"Yes. I understand that you may have a missing child in your coven."

Maggie listened, and Jesi shoved the paper with her notes under Maggie's tapping hand.

"So, William Shaw is part of your coven? Someone kidnapped two of our kids within the last week as well." Maggie paused. "Can you tell me what active power William has? Billy?"

Jesi tried to hear the other end of the conversation with no result.

"Really? Okay." Maggie wrote on the paper under her hand. She glanced at Jesi's writing.

"Can you give me the exact time he was taken?" She scribbled something down.

"Okay, and any evidence you could pick up before the police came to investigate?" Maggie wrote more. "Okay. I think the cases are related."

Jesi started nudging Maggie. Maggie looked at her, raising an eyebrow.

"Sylvia. They should talk to Sylvia," Jesi whispered.

"Yes. That sounds great. I'm going to give you the information for the head of our coven," Maggie said as she turned away and started talking away from the group. As much as Maggie trusted Chuck, she didn't at the same time.

Jesi picked up the sheet she handed to Maggie. She felt Chuck and Emma behind her. They all peered at the words.

"What time was he taken?" and "Do they have extra evidence?" were both written by Jesi. Underneath Maggie wrote "Billy. Reform rocks/crystals. 6:30 am. Dark aura, not quite human." Maggie's writing was barely legible.

"Now that you all have read the note, I guess we can safely say that our bad guy is looking for four elemental witches. He needs fire. I'm going to call Aunt Sylvia and start a call tree here and see what other covens we should contact." Maggie looked at the group.

"I brought a copy of the lab analysis of the dust with me." He pulled out a folded piece of paper and handed it to Maggie.

She looked over it. "Artemisia absinthium," Maggie said aloud. The tapping of her fingers started.

"What is that?" Emma asked. Chuck looked at Jesi. She shrugged. She wasn't familiar with that name.

"I think it's wormwood. We didn't pick that up with our analysis." Maggie pulled out her phone and typed something into it. "Yep, wormwood."

"That's pretty common," Jesi said.

"Yeah, but it doesn't fit with the other ingredients." Maggie tapped her fingers harder. Jesi shifted from foot to foot. She wanted to grab Maggie's hand and tell her to stop.

"But it reminds me of something I read once."

"Once?" Emma smirked.

"If I'm right, it would call for a lot of wormwood." Maggie stared into space. Jesi wanted to shake Maggie, to give them the information, but she knew Maggie.

Maggie didn't want to give out the wrong advice.

"Just tell us," Jesi said.

Maggie scrawled at her. "Fine," she answered. "Wormwood can be used in certain spells to help you control someone else."

"Okay, I'll start going through our orders again and make a list," Jesi said, "and I'll call the local shops and ask them to do the same."

"Great. I need to go to Aunt Sylvia's house." Maggie packed up her bag.

"What if the insurance company calls?"

"They should call my cell. And Jamie is coming this afternoon."

"Well, I'm with her," Emma said as she grabbed her own bag.

"Why aren't you working?" Jesi asked.

"It's Friday," Emma said. Jesi raised an eyebrow at her. "I'm working nights at the emergency vet office this week."

"It's Friday?" Jesi turned and looked at Chuck.

He nodded. Jesi frowned as she watched the other two ladies leave. Jesi turned to Chuck and leaned against the counter.

"Your lab has a pretty quick turnaround time."

"I might owe someone a favor." Chuck smiled at Jesi. Jesi grabbed his hand over the counter.

"Thank you for taking the supernatural seriously," Jesi said.

"Well, the break-in plus a security system materializing out of nowhere made everything real."

Jesi smiled back at him. She felt safe here with his hand in hers. No worries about gleaning into his past.

"But not the rock turning into a worm?" She teased.

"No. That happens every day," Chuck said. He leaned closer. "Can I ask you something?"

"Anything."

"You wouldn't miss this?" he asked.

"The magic?" she asked.

"Yeah, the magic," he said. "Being a witch."

"No. It has really turned my life upside down."

"You could do both. Just might have to practice a different type of law."

"What kind of law did you have in mind?" Jesi waggled her eyebrows and smiled.

She was almost nose to nose with Chuck. She looked down at his full lips and back to his blue eyes. He closed the distance and pressed his lips to hers. She inhaled his scent and licked his lips. Their tongues intertwined as his hand cupped the back of her neck. She grabbed his shirt and deepened the kiss.

Bells rang. Bells. Jesi pulled away and looked toward the door. A customer. One of the older ladies from the coven.

"Oh, don't mind me," she said as she made her way to the "Real Magic" room.

Chuck laughed. His deep rumble moved through her. Jesi laughed with him.

"I should go," Chuck said.

"Yeah. Probably a good idea." Jesi let go of his shirt. He took one of her hands in his.

"I'll call you," he said and kissed the back of the hand he held. He let her go and walked toward the door.

"You'd better," Jesi called.

"Bye, Jesi."

"Bye."

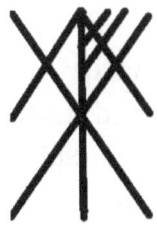

Chapter 11

Chuck sat back in his desk and looked over the files from the Macon kidnapping. It looked like a messier version of the two kidnappings here in town. He wanted to talk to the parents of the missing children again with the extra information he gained from these files. The scene in Macon had a clear point of entry, unlike the others. It also had the same dust found at the fourth scene, which he couldn't include in his report yet.

The entire prospect worried him. How many cases had he worked that involved magic? How many supernatural people or creatures or something had he put in jail? How was he supposed to refer to that group? Supernatural? Magical? Right now, that didn't matter.

He needed to concentrate. With absolutely no suspects, his focus deteriorated. He could start with the ingredients. He needed a list of all the shops in the drivable area that sold these herbs. All herbs. He knew at least two could be found at flower shops, grocery stores, and grown in people's yards. For all he knew, all of these could grow in anyone's yard.

He opened his pad and started listing shops he knew that sold special herbs. He had one shop on the list. He frowned at his pad. He would get a uniform cop to make some calls. He should re-interview the families and look over the scenes again with fresh eyes. Maybe he could get Jesi to go with him. His cell phone rang. He smiled as he looked at the name.

Jesi.

"Detective Massey." He didn't want the others around him to know who called.

"Hey, Chuck. It's Jesi."

"Hi. I'm glad you called." He felt a stupid grin flash on his face. Whenever he thought about her, he smiled. He'd never reacted that way towards another person. Maybe he didn't care what the others thought.

"Yeah?" Jesi asked.

"Yeah," Chuck said.

"I'm glad I called too," she said. He could hear her smile on the other end.

"What are you doing after lunch?" Chuck asked.

"Why, Detective, are you asking me to leave my post?" Jesi teased.

"Maybe." His voice softened.

"I'll talk to Maggie and get back to you," Jesi said.

"Excellent."

"I actually have something to tell you. About the case," Jesi said. She brought him back to the real world.

"Oh? Go ahead."

"After going through our purchase records," she said, "we have three people who bought the rare ingredients in the last month. Well, the last 6 months, really."

"That's great," he said. "Can you give me their names?"

"Yes. I have Sandy Smalls, Andres Marin, and Roger Hall."

"Roger Hall?" Chuck couldn't hide the surprise from his voice.

"Do you know him?"

"Is he tall, with dark hair?" Chuck asked. "Has a permanent smirk on his face and rolls his eyes like it's what keeps him breathing?"

"Yes," Jesi said. "That sounds like him."

"Yeah, he dates Hayley."

"How do you know Hayley?" Jesi asked.

"She's my sister." He let out a loud sigh.

"Hayley's your sister?" Jesi's voice caused Chuck to pull the phone away from his ear.

"Yeah, she's my sister," Chuck said.

"Sorry, I didn't mean to be so loud," Jesi said. "I'm just surprised. I should have put that together, because you are both Mr. Massey's kids."

"Yeah, I'm surprised she's dating Roger. He really rubs me the wrong way, but I don't think he would kidnap kids."

"I know what you mean. He's not really our favorite customer either," Jesi said. "I'm going to keep looking, but I don't know if the herbs are effective after six months. I just like being thorough."

"Well, you know more about that than I do, I'll trust your judgement." Chuck wrote the names down Jesi gave him.

"Why thank you, Detective."

"No problem, Councilor."

"You're such a sweet talker," Jesi said.

"You have no idea."

"Well, I look forward to finding out. I'll talk to Maggie and text you about this afternoon."

"Great. And I'm going to run these names through the system. I'll talk to you later. Bye."

"Bye."

~

The door slammed. The bells crashed against the frame. Jesi looked up and saw Maggie walk to the counter with several bags.

"What is that?"

"Research."

Jesi looked into the bags as Maggie heaved them onto the counter.

"Where did you get all these books?"

"Sylvia."

"No," Jesi said. "She let you take them off site?"

"They are from the library. Since we haven't fixed the door yet, I have to access them from her side." Maggie began to pull books out of the bags.

"And is she sending anyone to help us?"

"Yes." Maggie pulled a book off the top of one of the

piles. "Tomorrow. Someone is supposed to come help tomorrow."

"And what if we actually need to go after someone?"

Maggie looked at Jesi with eyebrows raised. "Are you saying you'll fight with me to get the kids back?"

"Of course. Why wouldn't I?" Jesi crossed her arms over her chest.

"Well, you're a lawyer and we might not be doing things that are super legal."

"Magic is also not something that you can take to court." She put her hands on her hips. She would not back down. She wanted to help those kids. She needed to help.

"Also, you've never been interested in this before," Maggie pointed out.

"I guess being so involved has changed things." Jesi sat down and looked at the books. Those kids were still missing. She wanted them to feel safe. Could she really help? "Thinking of those kids has really made me question what I've been doing with my life."

"Are you kidding? You've done great things. Your work in the legal field was great."

"But think of all the people I could put away with my gift."

"Your gift?" Maggie stilled. Jesi could feel her watching.

"Don't tease me." Jesi frowned.

"No tease. I'm just glad you're changing your tune about it being a curse." Maggie smiled at Jesi.

Jesi looked around the shop. As safe as she always felt in this shop, she never quite belonged. She looked different, and she didn't have magic. The itch in the back of her mind that told her she wasn't like the others was gone. She hadn't noticed when it left.

"I feel like I belong now," Jesi whispered to herself.

"Oh, honey. You've always belonged." Maggie hugged Jesi tight. "Does that mean you're going to get rid of the power stripping potion you carry around?"

"How do you know about that?" Jesi asked. Her heartbeat rose.

"I saw it in your bag the other week," Maggie said. "I decided you might act on it if I gave you a hard time."

"Have you told Sylvia?" Jesi asked. "And how did I miss gleaning that?"

"When's the last time you actively delved into the memories you pick up from me?" Maggie asked. She raised her eyebrows. "And I didn't tell Aunt Sylvia. Your secret is safe with me."

Jesi's heart slowed back down. She hadn't looked into Maggie's history. Each time they touched, Jesi let the memories wash over her. She absorbed them, but she ignored them. When did that start? Before Jesi could examine that thought, Maggie thrust a book into Jesi's hands.

"Look for any spells that include the ingredients from the dust, any that call for large amounts of wormwood, and any that require the elements," Maggie said as she sat down with a large tomb in front of her.

"What if someone comes in while we are looking?" Jesi asked.

"We stop and help them buy stuff." Maggie's matter-of-fact tone made Jesi smile.

"What if they are on the list?"

"Then we tackle them and make them talk."

"Make them talk?" Jesi wasn't sure she knew how to make someone talk.

"Sure. You can be Robert De Niro and I'll be Joe Pesci."

Jesi looked at Maggie as she flipped through the pages. "What if I want to be Joe Pesci?"

Maggie looked up with half a smile. "Alright, give me a good reason you should be Pesci."

Jesi stood up and shook her hair out of her face the best she could. Hands on hips, she said, "What? You think I'm funny? I'm a funny guy, huh?" She poked Maggie.

"Okay. You can be Pesci," Maggie said. "But lose the accent. That was terrible."

"It was excellent."

"Sure, it was. New York with a side of redneck." Maggie's smile was a million watts.

Jesi laughed as she sat back down. What would she do without Maggie when she went back to work? If she went back to work. She didn't think she could go back into corporate law. There had to be a place for her somewhere.

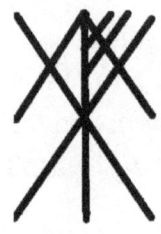

Chapter 12

Jesi joined Chuck in his SUV. They smiled at each other. Jesi felt a calm wash over her.

"So, who are we going to visit first?" Jesi asked.

He told her through text that he wanted to revisit the Nelson and Chambers' households and swing by Genevieve's if they get the chance. He hoped he would find something new based on the report sent from Macon.

"Actually, I wanted to visit Sandy Smalls first," Chuck said.

"Sandy Smalls?" Jesi asked. "You found her? We know what she looks like, but that's about it. We have no idea who she is other than her buying from the shop, and she doesn't do that often."

"If I'm right," Chuck said, "her name is Sandra Littlefield. She lives on the outskirts of Richmond Hill on the Ogeechee River."

Jesi took the sheet with Sandy's photo he held out.

"That's her," she said. "Should we call Maggie?"

"I don't think so," Chuck said. "The fewer people we have, the less likely they are to run."

Jesi thought about it. Technically, she knew how to deal with any magical foes. Of course, technically and prepared were two different realities. "Okay, but if I say we need to leave, we leave."

"Sure," Chuck said. "I'll handle the police side and you handle the magic side."

"And it was a man that attacked Amber," Jesi said. "He might have Sandy under his spell."

"Or Sandy might have him doing her bidding," Chuck said.

Jesi stared out the window and watched the trees go by for the rest of the drive. She never considered Sandy to be a threat, but Chuck was right. She could be pulling the strings. Looks are deceiving.

Thirty minutes later, they pulled up to a small house deep in the woods. You couldn't see it from the dirt road that led to it. The house itself looked like most other houses near the river. The ground floor was a garage and nothing else. This kept flooding from the river out of the second floor living area. Of course, that's only when a powerful hurricane isn't bearing down on the area.

Wildflowers filled the surrounding grounds. A vegetable garden grew off to the right and two big marigold bushes sat on each side of the stairs leading to the front door.

Chuck and Jesi walked up to the door and knocked. Inside, they heard a series of shushes and a glass item break. The door opened to reveal Sandy Smalls or Sandra Littlefield. Her thick black hair fell long down her back, but her eyes were a bright blue. Her face looked sun kissed. She wore a long skirt and a flowy top. She looked exactly the way Jesi remembered.

"Jesi," Sandy said, "and...?"

"This is Chuck," Jesi said.

"Detective Massey," Chuck said with a side eye to Jesi. "We were wondering if we could come in and talk?"

"What is this about, Officer?" Sandy asked.

She stood up straighter and pulled the front of her blouse closed over her chest. There was nothing to close, so Jesi thought it must be a habit.

"We are investigating the disappearances of some children," Chuck said. "We hoped you would help us."

Sandy opened her door wide. "Of course," she said. "I will help you. Come in quick."

She herded them in and pushed them through the hall and into the kitchen. She sat them down at the table and filled a kettle with water.

"I hope you like tea," she said. "It's really all I have."

"We love tea," Jesi said with no idea if Chuck liked tea or not, "but it's really unnecessary."

Sandy frowned a little.

"We would love some tea," Chuck said.

Sandy moved the kettle to the stove and turned it on. As she worked, Jesi heard knocks and the cabinets open and close behind the kitchen island where she couldn't see. It wasn't Sandy, as she was in full view.

Chuck looked at her and put a finger to his ear and

raised an eyebrow. Jesi nodded. Yes, she heard it too. When Sandy sat down at the table, Jesi still discerned little clicks and bumps from the kitchen.

"So, what is this about missing children?" she asked.

"Well, someone has kidnapped three magical children," Jesi said. She searched Sandy's face for any signs of surprise or shock or guilt. Sandy's mouth fell open, but she covered it with her hands.

"Three children?" she said. "How awful."

Jesi heard more sounds from under the cabinets. Chuck put his hand on his side where he kept his gun.

"We were wondering if you had heard anything about it," Chuck said.

"No!" Sandy rung her hands. "Those poor dears. I just can't bear to think about them. Kidnapped. Who kidnaps children?" She folded her hands in her lap. Lines appeared on her face that weren't there before. It looked like she aged twenty years. Tears rolled down her cheeks. "Those poor children," she whispered and closed her eyes.

Jesi looked at Chuck. His eyes were wide. He looked back and forth between her and Sandy and shrugged. Jesi walked over to Sandy and kneeled in front of her.

"Oh, Sandy," Jesi said. "Don't cry. We are going to find those children. We still need to ask you some more questions. Do you want us to give you a minute?"

Sandy nodded her head. Jesi moved to rub Sandy's back when something pushed her onto her butt. A small faery floated at face level. The naked light blue faery with long dark blue hair yelled at Jesi in a language that she didn't understand. The faery's little arms waved about. She pointed and gave Jesi a raspberry. The Fae flew back to Sandy and sat on her shoulder.

Sandy looked up at Jesi with enormous eyes. The lines in her face gone.

"You're the one that got Oblena's gift," she said.

Jesi nodded and looked over at Chuck. He stood, stunned with his gun out pointed at nothing and a variety of Fae surrounded him. They all looked at him, touched his hair and poked his nose. One of the Fae investigated the gun by crawling inside the barrel. Another danced on top of it. Jesi laughed despite herself.

"You look so scared," she said.

"Don't laugh," he said through clinched teeth. "What are these things?"

"They are faeries," Sandy said. "They live with me and we take care of each other."

"Are they going to hurt me?" Chuck whispered.

"They can," Jesi said, "and some types will, but I think they are just curious. If anyone is going to get hurt, it's me."

"Yes," Sandy said. "Oblena always asked before she touched me."

"I wasn't even thinking of that," Jesi said. "I'm so sorry. I just wanted to help you feel better." She carefully got up off the floor and made sure she didn't clobber a wandering Fae.

"Can you ask them to stop touching me?" Chuck asked.

"Oh, ladies," Sandy said. "He wants you to stop. Give

him space. Stop now." Sandy walked over and shooed the little faeries off. The kettle whistled. "You might as well put that gun away. It won't do you any good against them, unless your bullets are made of iron."

"I think I could use that tea now," Chuck said. He brought his gun down and shook it clear of faeries before he holstered it.

~

Chuck watched the faeries fly around the room as they helped Sandy get the tea together. They fascinated and scared him. Some of them didn't fly. They just hopped around on the counters and floor and helped where they could. Others stayed on her shoulders or in her hair. He knew, because one poked its head out each time she turned away from them.

They were all different colors. Blues, whites, pinks, grays, and he spied one that was violet. Some had on clothes, but most were naked. Sandy placed his tea in front of him. He picked it up and held it in his hands. The warmth helped calm him.

"How long have the Fae lived here?" Jesi asked.

"All my life," Sandy said. "Oblena knew, but few others venture out this far."

"Why?" Jesi asked. "If you don't mind me asking. The Fae generally don't pal around with humans."

"It's really not something I share," Sandy said. She side-eyed Chuck quickly. Jesi nodded at Sandy like she understood something he didn't.

"You know, Sandy," Jesi said, "I didn't properly introduce you. This is Detective Chuck Massey. He is my complement."

Chuck looked at Jesi in surprise. Did she tell everyone? Or was she using their connection to gain trust?

"Really?" Sandy said. One of the Fae flew to her and whispered in her ear. "Let's just say they are family."

"I respect that," Jesi said. "Will you tell us why you bought such a huge order of wormwood two months ago?"

Sandy smiled and stood up. "I'll do even better, I'll show you."

She rummaged around the kitchen and pulled out a jug and two glasses. "Here," she said, and poured a small amount for Jesi and Chuck.

Chuck picked up the glass and sniffed it. Vanilla and cloves overpowered his nose as well as the strong alcohol content. Jesi raised her glass to him and took a sip.

"Is this vermouth?" she asked.

Sandy smiled and put the jug away. "Yes," she said. "I make it myself. I usually grow my own wormwood, but I didn't grow enough this year. This lot drinks too much, so now I have to ration it."

Chuck took a sip. Vanilla, cloves, nutmeg, and something he couldn't place filled his tastebuds. The amount of alcohol in the sip overwhelmed him. He knew he wouldn't touch that stuff again.

"Do you mind if I have a look around?" Chuck asked.

"Not at all," Sandy said. "You look around and I'll

catch up with Jesi."

Jesi nodded at him, so he made his way through the house.

The small house didn't take long to search. Besides the kitchen, it had a living room, one bathroom, and two bedrooms. The attic held decorations, and art supplies filled the garage. She painted faeries. Of course, she did, he thought.

The grounds held little interest other than garden after garden. He had to admit they were beautiful. Given the options, he could stay here and relax all day. Otherwise, there was nothing here, unless she took to the water to hide the children, which was a possibility.

Chuck walked back to the house where Jesi and Sandy laughed. They both smiled at him.

"I think that's all we need from you," he said.

"If you need any help," Sandy said, "let me know."

"We will," Jesi said.

Sandy reached out and patted Jesi on the hand before Jesi stood up and followed him out.

Once in the car and down the road Chuck looked over at Jesi. "She let you glean her?" he asked. "That's what you call it, right? Glean?"

"She did," Jesi said. "And yes, it's glean. Sandy is clean. She legitimately made that vermouth."

"So, what did she mean when she said that the faeries are family?" he asked.

"Well, let's just say that Sandy isn't completely human," Jesi said. "And that's about as much as I can tell you without breaking her trust."

"Do you think she will be able to help us?" Chuck asked.

"Not really," Jesi said. "She's not a fighter, but she said she'd look through some of the books she has and keep her ears open for any news. She's older than she looks."

"Her file says she's 40," Chuck said.

"She's older than that," Jesi said. "Much older."

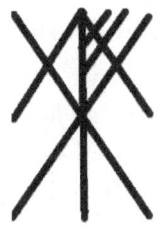

Chapter 13

Jesi sat down in a downtown coffee shop. The table stood next to a window overlooking Chippewa Square. After talking with the parents of the missing children, Chuck said they needed a break and suggested coffee. This was her favorite coffee shop. It was close to the law office where she used to work. Chuck sat down across from her and put her drink order in front of her.

"So, you like the locally owned places?" Jesi asked. She picked up her drink and inhaled the scent of the dark roast.

"Yeah," Chuck said. "I like supporting local businesses. I especially like it here. The art is always amazing."

Jesi looked at the art adorning the wall. The Gallery Espresso always hung local artists' work on the walls. If you liked it, you could buy it. They changed the art out regularly.

"Have you ever bought any of the art?" Jesi asked.

"No." Chuck sipped his coffee, closed his eyes, and sighed.

A slight smile graced his lips, and he sat back in his chair. He looked like he belonged in this café. Jesi never drank her coffee in the shop, always getting her fix to go.

"I feel like we didn't get much from our talks with the parents," Jesi said. She worried they wasted time, instead of researching.

Chuck opened his eyes and smiled at her. "But it helps the families know we are still focused on the case. If they think of anything, they will call now that they know we haven't given up. Sometimes, showing someone you care is worth the effort."

"They all gave us a look," Jesi said.

"Yeah?"

"Yeah. They all pulled me aside and wanted to know who you are to me," she added. It became increasingly apparent that they were connected throughout the day. They were never more than three feet apart when she wasn't pulled aside by the family. Even then she could feel which direction he was in with relation to herself. She noticed herself touching his arm or side more and more as the day progressed. He touched her more as well. Each graze spread warmth through her body. By the end of the day, that warmth had turned red hot.

"And?"

"I don't know. But I'd like to figure it out."

"Me too. But I'm worried it might be the stress of the situation talking. As much as I liked last night and as much as I want to do it again, I think we should slow down. I don't want to lose focus on the task at hand. We need to concentrate on finding the children. And then figure out us."

Jesi shook her head. "I have to disagree. I've been in plenty of stressful situations and they never felt like this." She reached over and folded her hand over his and squeezed.

"Hayley," Chuck said sharply.

"Charles."

Jesi looked up to see Hayley stand over Chuck with her arms crossed over her chest. She let go of his hand.

"I see you are chatting up the girl from the magic shop," Hayley sneered.

"I see you are still with Mr. Manipulative," Chuck replied.

Jesi looked around and saw Roger in line for coffee.

"Roger is twice the man you are." Hayley's face twisted with rage.

Chuck's expression was blank. Cold. Jesi felt chills down her arms.

"Right," Chuck said. "Dad said you got a tattoo."

Jesi looked between the two. She didn't think about it before, but the only thing they had in common was their eye color. Chuck didn't really favor Alan, but Hayley was the spitting image of her father.

"He's not your dad," Hayley spat at Chuck.

His blank expression twitched ever so slightly. Jesi suddenly didn't want to see Chuck lose control.

"Well, let's see it," he said.

"No." Hayley pursed her lips and lifted her chin as if

she'd won the verbal sparring match.

Chuck's nose flared.

"I want to see it," Jesi intervened with a small smile. "Maggie says it looks great."

Hayley looked at Jesi with a smirk. "Learn some manners from your girl, Charles."

She pulled her dark blonde hair up from her neck and turned to show Jesi. Chuck leaned in to see.

"It looks lovely," Jesi lied. It looked like a capital X with an arrow pointing up, creating a third line down the middle of the X. "Absolutely perfect for you."

Roger chose that moment to show up and kissed Hayley's neck. She dropped her hair. Roger stood about six inches taller than Hayley, and she wasn't exactly short. His dark hair almost hung into his eyes and his eyes attempted to smolder into every girl's onlooking gaze. Hayley reached up and brushed her fingers over the stubble on his jawline. He wore a permanent smirk on his handsome face that Jesi had an urge to punch since the day she met him.

"What happened to your arm?" Jesi asked. Hayley's arm had a swatch of gauze taped over her wrist area. Jesi reached out to touch Hayley's arm. Hayley snatched it back and scowled at Jesi.

"Some brat kid bit me in class. I swear, they need to let me teach the older students. I'm done with the small ones." She shook her head and pursed her lips into a deep frown. "Anyway." And with a roll of her eyes, Hayley walked out the door.

"I'm watching you," Chuck said to Roger.

"Sure, you are," Roger said. He moved to follow Hayley.

"Wait," Jesi said. She stood up quickly. "I was wondering if you could..."

Jesi fell forward mid-sentence and knocked the table down with her. She reached as she fell, but only brushed her hand on the bottom of Roger's jacket. Chuck pulled her up into her chair and she could only sit and watch as Roger left with a smirk that was smirkier than normal. It was the perfect target for her fist, she decided.

Jesi turned to Chuck. "That was a lovely family reunion," she said.

Chuck righted the table. She had coffee all over herself, but it appeared that Chuck escaped her clumsy moment.

"Sorry about that," Jesi said.

An employee came over and handed her a towel to help her dry off and began mopping up the floor.

"What were you thinking?" Chuck asked.

"I thought that this was the perfect chance to find out if Roger is involved," Jesi whispered.

Chuck shook his head and smiled. She reached across the table and squeezed his hand. Chuck's attention drifted outside, back to his sister and her slimy boyfriend.

"I just don't know what she sees in him," Chuck said. He squeezed Jesi's hand back.

"She's young," she offered. "We don't always make the best decisions at that age."

Chuck shook his head and sighed. "We all thought she was going to marry her high school sweetheart,

Pablo. I called him Paul. I know that it's not always the best idea, but we all loved him. They were great together. Then, all of a sudden, he began acting strangely and just disappeared. I never told her, but I tracked him down about nine months ago up in North Carolina. He was in a terrible place, mentally. I offered to help, but he turned it down. Said he needed time to figure some things out. I left. I try to keep tabs on him, but he dropped off the radar six months ago. I don't think he's coming back. Hayley met Roger around the same time I located Paul, and she started to change."

Chuck studied their clasped hands. "You know she is the one who's supposed to take over the auto shop? She's a brilliant mechanic. That never intimidated Paul, but somehow, Roger convinced her to step away from it and become a teacher. She's a substitute. She doesn't have the credentials to be certified. As far as I know, she's not trying to become a full-time teacher."

"What exactly does Roger do?" Jesi asked. "He comes by the shop, as you know, but we have no clue what he actually does."

"He works in sales for a business that sells insurance," Chuck said with a frown. "I think it's a cover for something more nefarious, but I don't have proof. He's either legit or very good at covering his tracks."

Jesi thought about the situation. She never liked Roger and agreed that he was not a good person, just from the way he treated her and Maggie at the shop. But she knew the danger of assumptions from her time as a lawyer.

"When we find those children," she said, "I'll help you find the truth about Roger, assuming he's not actually involved."

She squeezed Chuck's hand again and nodded. He smiled and lifted her hand and kissed her knuckles. It burned her right to her core. A breath hitched in her throat. She smiled and felt her stomach flip. She would be in a world of hurt if he was no longer interested when they found the missing children. She was pretty sure he'd stolen her heart.

"Let's go," Chuck said. "You need to get out of those wet clothes."

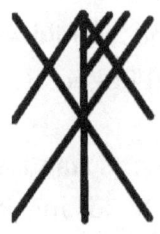

Chapter 14

Chuck walked Jesi to her door. He thought about his sister and how he could pull her away from the man who currently had her wrapped around his finger. He shook his head and focused on Jesi. Her hair reflected the light in the hallway. He loved how it looked both wild and tamed all at once.

As they questioned the families, it gave him a chance to see a different side of her. She was open and honest when she communicated with the grieving families. The sympathy she showed brought out a trust in the coven members that he couldn't do with this group. Even while she resisted the offered handshakes and hugs, he could tell it hurt her to decline.

She unlocked her door and turned to look at him over her shoulder. He smiled down at her. Those dark blue eyes would be the death of him.

"Do you want to come in?" she asked. Her soft smile melted the shield he tried to keep erect all day.

"I really shouldn't," he said.

"Of course, you should," she said.

"It's already so complicated." He ran his hand through his hair.

"It's always going to be complicated," Jesi replied. She took his hand and guided him inside.

"You're twisting my arm," he said, though he followed with zero resistance.

She closed, then locked the door, and led him to her couch. The one where they shared their first kiss.

"You wait here, while I change out of these coffee-stained clothes," Jesi said.

Chuck looked around the place. He didn't take the chance to look around the day before. His attention stayed on Jesi the entire time. The small apartment had little on the walls. The bookshelf in the tiny dining area had more books than it could hold, and legal journals cluttered the end table. Jesi walked back into the room wearing leggings and a long white t-shirt and sat down beside him. She looked more enticing in the plain outfit than she did wearing her business suit.

"I'm sorry for causing such a fiasco at the coffee shop," she said. It was the fifth time she'd apologized.

"Again," he said, "there is no need to apologize." She smiled at his words and took his hands in hers.

"You can always say no, but I think you need a little time to relax," Jesi said. "The coffee shop didn't offer much of that."

"No," he agreed. "Not today."

"And to be honest," she said. "I'm distracted being

near you. Kids or not, you are my biggest distraction. And Maggie once told me that sometimes our brains need something it can solve. I think we can take a bit of time and solve a little of us tonight."

She placed her hand on his cheek and traced her fingers around his jawline. He couldn't think of a counterargument. He wanted to understand the connection between them. He spent the day by her side, touching her arm, leading her by putting his hand on the small of her back, and guiding her by the elbow. Each time he felt the tingle and warmth through his body. It lingered the more time he spent with her. Was it real? Was it stress? Would the attraction and desire and spark continue to burn after they relieved some tension?

"I don't want you to do something you're not ready for," he said.

"I'm ready," she said and placed a soft kiss on his lips. "Are you ready?"

"Oh, yes I am," he said and wrapped his hands around her waist and pulled her onto his lap.

His lips crashed into hers. The hard kiss of desperate exploration sent electricity down his spine. Her hands moved into his hair. His hands found their way up under her t-shirt onto the soft skin of her back. She licked and sucked his lips before kissing down his jaw and onto his neck. He felt her legs circle his waist and her teeth nibbled his ear. Eyes rolled in the back of his head. A moan escaped him. He felt his cock grow harder with each rub from Jesi's pelvis. He pushed her back to look into her flushed face. A warm pink filled her cheeks, her eyes hooded, and he pulled her in for another hard kiss. One hand moved onto the back of her neck, while the other moved down to grab her round ass. He'd snuck peeks at this ass for days. She was perfect.

Jesi pulled open his shirt. Lost buttons would be a problem for the morning, but now, he wanted to take her shirt off too. Everyone needed to maintain an equal amount of clothing. It was more fun that way. He lifted her shirt over her head to see her beautiful full breasts trapped by a black bra. It was his turn to nuzzle her neck. With hands wrapped around her back, he licked and kissed down her neck and collarbone until he came to those full breasts. He maneuvered his hand to unclasp her bra. As soon as it fell, his mouth was over one of her nipples. Her gasp echoed in his head. His tongue swept and flicked at her hardened pebble. Her moans grew louder, and she rubbed against him faster.

~

Jesi could barely contain herself. She lifted his face up and looked into his eyes. They were full of lust and desire, more so than anyone before. She kissed him again. With swollen lips, she fed her need to be close to him.

"Bedroom," she said between kisses.

Before she could stand, he pulled her tight against him and picked her up. He held on to her ass while she locked her legs around his waist. The bed stood a short distance away in the small apartment. Once at the bed, he dropped her down on the mattress and tugged at her leggings. With no time at all, he pulled them down into a pile on the floor.

He kissed her knees and made his way up her body. A nibble followed each kiss. Each scrape of his teeth caused an ache deep in her core. She felt his stubble with each kiss and rub. He hovered over her mound and kissed her through her panties and rubbed his face there. He looked wild and free. She squirmed and panted at his touch. Then he licked her clit through the cotton fabric. She moaned and knew he could feel how wet her panties were, how wet she was, but he continued upward to her belly button, between her breasts, each nipple, and finally, back to her mouth that welcomed him greedily.

Jesi ran her hands down his chest. You couldn't tell how strong he was until his shirt came off. He held himself above her, nibbling at her lips and neck. She felt his muscles ripple beneath her hands as they made their way down to his slacks and undid his belt. The pants came next. She pushed down his pants and underwear all at once. She felt his hard cock spring to life. He twitched when she wrapped her hand around it, sliding her fist up and down.

His eyes gazed into hers. She smiled at him, then licked the side of his mouth. His deep moan vibrated through her. She couldn't wait. She pushed down her own panties and pulled him to her. Arms and legs wrapped around his body. They kissed each other wildly, teeth and tongues clashed, desperate still.

Chuck broke away. "Are you sure about this?" he panted out. Jesi laughed.

"Yes," she said.

With a smooth movement, she pushed him so she was on top, straddling him. His smooth muscular skin beneath her begged for her touch. She ran her hands over his shoulders and pecs, admiring the color differences of their skin. His hands ran over her legs and stomach. She leaned over to her nightstand, rummaged around, and pulled out a box of condoms.

"You always have those around?" he asked with a smirk.

"I like to be prepared," she said with a smile.

"Sexy, smart, and responsible. My kind of woman."

He took the box from her and pulled out a condom. Taking it out of the package, he held his hard cock pointing up between her legs and slowly slid down the condom. Jesi never knew that putting on contraception could be so sexy. She placed a hand over his and stroked him a few more times. His other hand reached up and massaged one of her breasts. It sent shocks down her body right to her clit when he brushed her nipple. As if he could read her mind, he took the other hand and pressed his thumb on that bundle of nerves and rocked it back and forth. It set her on fire. She trembled.

Jesi took hold of his hands before she exploded in pleasure and placed them above his head on the mattress. She kissed him once again and lifted herself up. Ever so slowly, she eased back down. The head of his cock slid into her wet pussy. They gasped in unison. Her eyes rolled in the back of her head with pleasure. His girth stretched her wide, but she continued to plunge herself and savored the sensation.

"Oh God," he whispered when at last he filled her.

She stared into his blue eyes. They pierced into her soul.

"I want to touch you," he said.

She let go of his hands, and they caressed her sides and bottom. She moved then. Up and down. Each movement sent shock waves up her spine. He took hold of her hips and they moved together. With each thrust and buck, they moved faster and faster. Her head sank into the crook of his neck. She panted each time he entered her. Her entire body crackled with electricity. She felt his lips on her neck, then on her earlobe, and a heavy deep moan reverberated down to her core. She was ready, but she couldn't speak. She moved her head to look in his eyes.

"Oh, Jesi," he whispered.

She exploded around him. Her own cries echoed in the room. He pulled her tight, and she felt his own release. They continued to move together slowly as they drew out the last bits of pleasure from each other. Their eyes never wavered. Jesi thought she saw sparks move between his eyes with each lingering tremor.

At last, Jesi collapsed next to Chuck. Propped on her side, she moved her fingers up and down his arm. She felt the sparks from their connection. Chuck wrapped his arm around her and pulled her closer. He rubbed his nose on hers and placed light kisses on her lips.

"Do you think we solved anything?" Chuck asked.

"Yes," Jesi said. She ran her fingers through his hair.

"What do you think?"

"Yes," Chuck said.

She felt his hand rub up and down her back. Warmth and energy spreading out across her body at his constant touch.

"What do you think we solved?" she asked.

"Whether we could walk away from each other," he said. She furrowed her brow. "I think you're stuck with me now."

Jesi laughed. "I think I can bear the load."

Chapter 15

Jesi walked into the shop the next morning. Maggie looked up from the counter, then down at her watch, and tutted at Jesi.

"What?" Jesi asked.

"You are late," Maggie said.

Her purple hair was flat in the front and sticking up in the back, like she didn't brush it. The dark circles under her eyes showed just how little sleep she got.

"I'm usually late," Jesi said. "So are you."

"Exactly." Maggie put books into a bag. "If you were late when you worked over at that fancy law office, they would dress you down. And don't deny it."

"That's true, but this has never been an issue before." Jesi moved cautiously through the store.

"Yes, and we've spent a year with nothing important happening. Kids are missing now. And I need you here. Aunt Sylvia just called. She thinks she's found the right book, so I'm going over there." Maggie picked up two of the four bags she brought in the day before.

"I hate to do this to you, but please, keep looking through those books and watch over the shop. I shouldn't be long. And try not to get distracted by Detective Hottie."

"What?" Jesi asked, taken aback. Maggie was never this short.

"Really? You're going to 'what' me?" Maggie said.

"Yes. What?" Jesi asked.

She stood up straighter. She would not put up with the attitude Maggie was throwing her way. They had too much respect for each other to act this way.

"Just don't take any impromptu dates again until I get back," Maggie said.

"It wasn't a date."

"Sure," Maggie said as she opened the door.

"I called you," Jesi said. "We talked about Sandy Smalls and how Chuck and I were going to talk to Anabelle, Judy, and Genevieve."

"Oh, that's right," Maggie said. Her face drew tight with a frown. "What did you learn?"

"Nothing we didn't already know," Jesi said. "Chuck wanted to compare the crime scenes with the one in Macon. He knew it would be easier to get cooperation if I came along. Genevieve agreed to let him file a report on the attempted kidnapping. And he sent me a message this morning. Andres Marin is out of the country. He's been in Spain for a month."

"Okay. Well, keep me posted. I'll be back." Maggie's frown didn't disappear. She juggled the bags in her hands.

"Hey. There's something else bothering you, isn't there?"

"Yes, it's just..." Maggie sighed. "Gigi did all of this before. I was always right there with her. So, now that she's gone, people expect me to pick up where she left off. I'm just not sure I'm the right person for the job." Maggie looked defeated.

Jesi studied her closely. The bags slacked in her hands, her eyes were dim, and her shoulders hunched. The Maggie Jesi knew was fading.

"You're the perfect person for the job, Maggie," Jesi said. "I have your back."

Maggie smiled softly at Jesi and left the shop.

Jesi sat down behind the counter and looked at the stack of books. What was she going to do with all of this? Maggie might not feel like the right person for the job, but Jesi never felt like the right person for the job when it came to magic. The doubts kept coming back. She wondered if it would always be like this. Confident one minute and insecure the next. The power stripping potion burned a hole in her pocket. She promised to not take the potion, but it was a crutch at this point. She liked the option, as terrible as that sounded.

She stared at the rack in front of her. It held small bags of herbs and teas. It was the one they cobbled together after the break-in. It remained in terrible shape, but the three of them rebuilt it. That poor rack could collapse at any moment. It was doing the best it could. Just like Jesi. Just like Maggie.

Jesi sighed. She compared herself to a shelving rack.

She shook her head and opened the closest book.

~

Bells rang from the shop door as Jesi closed the second book. No one had come to the shop that morning, and Jesi could use some socializing. She looked up to see Hayley coming toward the counter. Her dark blonde hair was long down her back. Her face didn't look happy to be there. Jesi took a deep breath.

"Welcome to Herbs and Healing." She smiled at Hayley. "Can I help you?"

Hayley looked at Jesi with her lips pursed and her arms crossed over her chest.

"I need to pick up some things for Roger."

The eye roll was uncalled for. It appeared as though she still didn't enjoy visiting the shop. Jesi bent down and started going through the bags of pre-ordered goods. She found none with Roger's name; she stood up. Hayley held a list out to Jesi between two lax fingers.

"Okay," Jesi said and grabbed the paper.

"Just hurry," Hayley spat.

Jesi smiled at Hayley. The little shit. It was the same smile she used in the courtroom. Being southern and a lawyer helped Jesi perfect the nice/nasty smile. Her mother always told her to 'kill them with kindness'.

She looked at the list and grabbed a bag as she walked onto the shop floor. She nearly dropped everything in front of the crooked rack of herbs. The list contained everything from Maggie's analysis of the black powder plus a pound of wormwood. A pound. The last order from Roger also requested a pound, which Hayley picked up two days ago. Jesi took a deep breath. It couldn't be a coincidence. She steadied her hands and pulled the herbs she could off the shelf on the shop floor and then headed to the "Real Magic" room.

"We store the more controlled herbs in the staff room. Just give me a minute."

"I thought the staff room was over here." Hayley pointed to the room behind the counter.

"Oh no, this one. Employee's only." Jesi pointed at the sign.

"That says 'Real Magic'."

Jesi looked at Hayley, then at the sign, then back at Hayley.

"So, it does." Jesi disappeared inside the room.

Once inside, Jesi pulled her phone out of her pocket and texted Maggie.

"It's Roger," she texted with a picture of the list attached.

She started pulling the last of the ingredients from the bins. The phone dinged.

"Don't give him the wormwood," Maggie replied.

Jesi looked at the wormwood bin. It was extremely low. Two ounces at best.

"We only have 2 oz left. He picked up a lb 2 days ago," Jesi sent back. She glanced at the closed door as she fumbled with the bag. Ding.

"Perfect. Give him the 2 oz and slip a tracking stone in the bag."

Jesi stared at the text. Really? That was a desperate mom spell. She had never used a tracking spell. She didn't know where to begin and Hayley was waiting. And did Maggie think she would intrude on someone's privacy? Yep. She was a lawyer willing to do anything to get those kids back.

"Words," Jesi sent back.

"'Mark this object, we will find, far away, at another time'."

"Vague," Jesi texted.

"Your face is vague. Now, do it," Maggie's message read.

Jesi rolled her eyes and grabbed a rock from one of the displays. Focusing, she repeated the words in a whisper. The stone heated in her hand and just as quickly cooled. She dropped it in the bag, shook it to the bottom, and placed the wormwood on top.

She walked out of the room and over toward Hayley who was looking at her phone having not moved.

"Okay," Jesi began, "I have everything here, only we don't have enough wormwood. I can only give you two ounces right now."

"What? Only two ounces? He needs a pound," Hayley practically yelled.

Jesi looked at Hayley with wide eyes. Hayley white knuckled her phone. She looked ready to throw it.

"He purchased a pound a few days ago. We haven't had a chance to restock," Jesi said.

"Unbelievable," Hayley huffed.

Jesi slid around Hayley. "I'll give you the two ounces

for free and give Roger a call when we restock the wormwood," Jesi said as she finished adding up the order.

After she made change out of the temporary cash box because of the broken cash register, Jesi handed the money over to Hayley and touched her hand lightly. Jesi needed to get a glean from Hayley.

The images flowed to her. They were dark. Dark eyes and hooded figure. Hayley's tattoo. But it was different. The lines formed a diamond shape on three legs, unlike the large x with an arrow in the middle. And it ended too soon. Something felt wrong. Jesi needed more. She just needed two seconds.

Hayley had already turned away. Jesi followed her and grabbed her elbow. Her mind flooded with images. All jumbled, unlike the chronological images of everyone else. She fought through the influx of information and chaos.

"Can I see your tattoo again?" Jesi bit out.

She breathed hard as she focused on the hooded figure. He was applying the tattoo. The hood melted away. Roger. His eyes glowed. The tattoo changed. Switching focus, she looked at the tattoo. It swerved and wavered, fading in and out, ending into a different tattoo than she saw before. More images took shape in her mind as she pulled her focus back to the present to see Hayley lifting her hair to show her that tattoo. It was the new design, not the one they saw yesterday. Not the one Roger applied in the glean.

"And what did you say it meant again? It's so pretty."

Hayley looked at Jesi and offered a slight smile. "Gift."

It was the first smile Jesi had seen from the girl in months. Jesi smiled at her as Hayley walked out the door. Once gone, Jesi ran back to the desk and drew the new tattoo design and wrote down everything she could put together from the jumbled glean. She was finishing the draft when her phone rang.

"Maggie. I have so much to tell you," Jesi said.

"You?" Maggie asked. "I have information too. Is Roger still there?"

"No. He didn't come. It was Hayley," Jesi explained.

"Is she still there?" Maggie asked.

"No. She left ten minutes ago."

"Ugh. Okay. Call Chuckers. I found the spell. And Hayley's a part of it," Maggie said.

"What?"

"Yeah," Maggie said, "Aunt Sylvia is calling a few people to help us. I'll be at the shop soon."

"Okay," Jesi said.

"Call Chuck. Bye, girl."

"Bye."

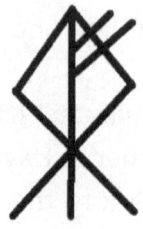

Chapter 16

Chuck was back in the shop listening to Jesi and Maggie go back and forth about the tattoo on Hayley's neck.

"I don't know what to tell you. It's just different," Jesi said. "I drew it right here. It has a diamond shape in it now and less vertical lines."

"I see that," Maggie said. "But how could it change? I realize it's a magical tattoo, but she just got it within the last week."

"Roger must have wanted to change it for some reason." Jesi didn't look convinced of her own statement.

"He wouldn't change it is the point," Maggie said. She pointed to the book she was holding. "I found the spell he's using. It's used to call forth a demon. Once the demon is out of the Underworld, it will grant the caster one request, and then the demon goes free. A demon free in the world can cause mass chaos or worse. That rune cluster is part of the spell. 'Gift' is written out in Norse runes, one letter on top of the next. He used the runes that spelled out 'gift' in English. Of course, it would make more sense if he used the Norse word for gift, but I can't argue with stupid."

"What if the new design spells something else?" Chuck asked.

Both ladies looked at him. Chuck shrugged. He was new to magic, but he knew that keeping a closed mind could be the end of an investigation. He was the fresh eyes they needed.

"Okay," Maggie said. "Now, we just need to figure out which letters are here. It might take a while. At least we know it will be in English."

"Yes, but we have two days, maybe less," Jesi said. "We need to concentrate on keeping all elemental fire witches safe."

"And finding my sister," Chuck said. She became top priority ten minutes ago.

"And you gleaned nothing else from Hayley?" Maggie asked for the third time.

"No." Jesi frowned. "She is definitely under a spell and she's been with the children, but backgrounds, locations, and normal actions are all jumbled. It's like her mind is in complete chaos."

"The tracking stone," Maggie said, eyes wide.

Jesi jumped up and started going through something under the counter. Chuck looked over the counter to watch Jesi toss papers out of the shelves.

"Stop. I'll find the map," Maggie said, pushing Jesi out of the way. "You go get a pendulum."

"Right." Jesi rushed on to the shop floor. Chuck

followed. He had no idea what she was looking for, but he wanted to help.

"I can't believe you don't have your own pendulum," Maggie called from the room behind the counter.

"Icantbelieve mummumum," Jesi mimicked Maggie under her breath.

"What are you looking for exactly?" Chuck began looking through the shelves.

"A pendulum," Jesi said.

She pulled a blue pointed rock off the shelf with a long gold chain attached to the end. Chuck raised an eyebrow and slowly nodded his head. He would wait for a better explanation.

Maggie laid out a map of Savannah and the surrounding areas on a workbench in the workshop. She looked over her shoulder at them as they entered the room.

"Are you ready?" she asked.

"Do I have to be the one to do this?" Jesi asked. She was worried she would do this wrong.

"Yes, you put the spell on the rock," Maggie said. She pulled Jesi over to the table.

Jesi took a deep breath and bit her lip. "Okay." She stood next to the table and let the blue rock dangle over the map while holding the end of the chain. She closed her eyes and gently swayed the rock over the map in an increasing circle.

"What exactly is she doing?" Chuck whispered to Maggie.

"She's using a pendulum, or pointed crystal on a

string, to find the location of the rock she spelled earlier today," Maggie said.

"That is not helping," Chuck said. "Don't they use pendulums in construction?"

"Yes, they do, but not the same way we use them. Today, Jesi put a tracking spell on an object. Now, she is using that pendulum with her magic to find that object on the map. It's a simple locator spell, but much more specific since the magic on the object will respond directly to the caster."

The crystal spun quickly and landed on a spot on the map. It landed on a busy corner in Southside, Savannah.

"I think there's a CVS there," Chuck said, studying the map.

"I think you're right," Jesi said.

"Fuck," Maggie said. "Okay. Let's try again in half an hour unless you want to risk them not being there when we get there. We need a final destination. We need to find those kids." Maggie ran her hand through her hair and started tapping her fingers on the bench.

"Okay," Chuck said, "I will start driving that way and you can call me with an updated address. I can watch the location for anything suspicious."

Jesi and Maggie looked at each other. "I don't know if we can protect you from here," Jesi said.

Chuck balked. "Protect me?" he asked. "I'm a police officer. A detective. I've been beaten and shot. I have a bullet wound on my ass. I can take Roger."

"But he's a witch. A dark witch," Jesi said. "He won't play by your rules. He doesn't even play by our rules. We don't even know what his active power is."

"You're really worried," Chuck said.

"Yeah. I don't want you to get hurt," Jesi said.

She frowned up at him. Chuck felt the same way about her. He would rather put himself in danger over her.

"What if I promise not to engage?" he asked.

Jesi took a deep breath. Maggie started tapping her fingers again.

"I won't be able to stop you, huh?" Jesi asked.

"Not likely."

Chuck rubbed Jesi's arms and gave her a soft smile. Her face softened, and she smiled back.

"Just be safe and stay back." She leaned forward and kissed him on the cheek. "Let us know when you get there."

Chuck nodded and left. He felt his chest tighten as he walked away from her. This situation was getting more dangerous, and Jesi was determined to be right in the middle. He knew he had met his match. She wouldn't back down, just like him. Only she was probably safer in this magical world than him. She may have the upper hand with the magic end of things, but he knew what to do on a stakeout. They would find Roger's location and from there, the missing kids and his sister.

~

Chuck called Jesi. He sat outside of the CVS in Southside.

"Chuckers," a voice answered.

"Maggie." Chuck rolled his eyes.

"Jesi is using the pendulum now. Do you see anything?"

"No," he said. "I've driven around this two-block radius. I don't see Hayley or Roger's car. I'm staring at the CVS entrance right now, in case one of them comes out."

"Wow," Maggie said. "We need more police friends, especially if you all cover your bases like you."

"A perfect world this is not," Chuck replied.

"Sour," Maggie said. "You shouldn't have the same opinion about your profession as I do."

Chuck could hear Jesi talking in the background. Maggie's muffled voice came through as well. He couldn't make out what they were saying.

"Chuck," Jesi said through the phone.

He couldn't help himself. He smiled at the sound of her voice.

"I'm here," he answered. *I'm here*, he thought. He wanted to be there for her always.

"She should still be there," she said. "In the CVS. The location has not changed."

"How accurate is this spell?" he asked. "Could they be within 100 feet or a mile or anything?"

"It's pretty accurate. More like 10 feet," she said.

Damn, he thought. That's one hell of a spell.

"I'll go inside and look around," he said. "Keep doing what you are doing every five to ten minutes and call me if the location changes."

"I will. Bye."

"Bye."

He ended the call and grabbed a hat from the passenger side. He didn't have much to disguise himself from Hayley. He'd only met Roger a handful of times, so he hoped Roger wouldn't recognize him if he wore a Savannah Bananas hat. Once he exited the car, he headed for the entrance.

The bright florescent lights were hard on his eyes. People mulled around the store, gathered items in baskets, and read labels. No one looked familiar. No one looked his way. The Saturday afternoon crowd just wanted to be home instead of friendly. Even people in the south had their limits to niceties.

He left the store and turned left to walk the perimeter of the building. A brown paper bag caught his eye. It was near the Redbox on the side of the store. The bag said WATKINS in big red letters. He pulled out his phone.

"Hey. They haven't moved. Did you find them?" Jesi asked.

"No," he said. "I haven't found them. But I'm looking at a brown paper bag labeled 'Watkins'."

"Really?" Jesi said. "There is a bag with your name on it at the CVS." He could hear Maggie curse in surprise. "She wants to know what's in it."

"She wants me to open something that is a potential magical bomb?" he asked.

"Yeah. Hold on." Jesi relayed his question.

"Maggie says that considering the spell he is setting up is within 48 hours, there is no way he would waste energy to set up a magical bomb for her."

"So, open it." He eyed the small bag.

"Please, trust us. Trust me," Jesi said.

Her voice sounded confident and strong. Chuck pressed his lips together. Could he trust this woman? Her soft curls and blue eyes came to mind. The strength behind those eyes and the confidence in her step had him nodding to himself. Yes, he trusted her. He reached out and grabbed the bag from the ledge and opened it. A small blue rock sat in the bag's bottom with a note.

"There is a small blue rock in the bottom of the bag with a note," he said.

"That's the rock I put in Hayley's bag," Jesi said. "What does the note say?"

"It says 'Check'."

He heard Jesi repeat it to Maggie. A loud "SON OF A BITCH" rang in his ear. A door slammed.

"Sounds like she's not taking it well," he said.

"No. I'd say not." Jesi sighed. "Thank you so much for going out there. I really appreciate it. We really appreciate it."

"I'd do it again for you," Chuck heard himself say. He was more attached than he realized, because he would absolutely do it again.

"What? Oh," Jesi said. "Maggie says to leave the bag."

"Why?" Chuck looked at the bag in his hand.

"The longer they think it's taken us to find the bag, the better." Jesi lowered her voice. "She just said something about checking his little pecker. I need to go calm her down. I'll talk to you later."

"Okay, I'll call you or come by later," he said.

"I like that plan."

Chuck smiled into the phone as he put the bag back on the ledge. "Bye."

Chapter 17

"What we need is a computer program to do this for us," said Jesi.

"It would take longer for us to code the program than just doing this by hand," Maggie replied. She was in the workshop getting ingredients organized. They'd been working for hours and everything blurred together.

"What's all involved with that reversal spell you're putting together?" Jesi asked.

"Well," Maggie said, "First, I am putting something together to counteract the hold he has on Hayley. I'm increasing the size, in case he put the same hold on the kids. The counter spell will affect everyone, not just the closest person. Then, I'm going to put together a kit to stop the summoning spell mid-spell. Then, I'm going to put together a kit to send the demon back if we don't stop it in time. Then I'll write out the words that go with each spell pouch."

"Why don't you give the words to the witches

coming with us and let them do it without the casting ingredients?" Jesi asked.

"I'm not sure there is anyone strong enough to do these spells without the casting ingredients," Maggie said. "It's very complex and pulls a lot of energy from the caster. We have so few members who are trained and willing to go into a magical battle. Those near the strength to pull this off are too old or freeze under pressure."

"Who freezes under pressure?" Jesi asked.

"Aunt May."

"Ooh. She does freeze under pressure," Jesi said. "Remember when she yelled at us for playing near the bathroom at Gigi's?"

Jesi waited for Maggie to look at her as they both said, "I HAVE PERFORMANCE ANXIETY."

Jesi laughed with Maggie. She remembered that day. The two girls were playing in the house. The two of them no older than six when Aunt May threw open the door, telling them to stop playing near the bathroom. "I have performance anxiety" was an inside joke the two of them shared. Once Jesi grew up, she understood more about where Aunt May was coming from and felt bad for laughing. As a six-year-old, she didn't know better.

"Poor Aunt May. She's not in the state right now anyway and refuses to try the teleport spell," Maggie said as she measured more ingredients.

"I don't blame her," said Jesi. "What if she leaves half of herself?"

"What is this? Star Trek?" Maggie asked as she

combined the herbs.

"I wish," Jesi said. "I wonder if Chuck likes Star Trek?"

"I wonder if Chuckers would want to learn any of this?" Maggie asked.

"Only if you stop calling him Chuckers."

"Ha. Never. Chuckers for life. I'm going to get him a shirt that says that," Maggie laughed.

Jesi rolled her eyes. She needed to figure out what the runes on Hayley's neck spelled when stacked on top of one another. Per the spell Maggie was ninety-nine percent sure Roger was using, the word could only have up to 4 letters. And since she didn't need the exact order, she would need to try thousands of combinations and several overlapped. Jesi was sure she couldn't count that high at the moment. She thought she could learn to code and write a program to figure this out long before she could do it by hand. It was really an impossible task. How would she ever figure this out?

"And no word from Vera?" Jesi asked.

"Nope," Maggie said. "It is really hurting us that the coven tracker and rune expert is working in England. She hasn't returned my calls or texts in over a week. I'd be worried, but this isn't the first time she's been MIA for over a week. Here, these are all the spells written out just in case." Maggie handed her a small stack of papers.

"Covering your bases?" Jesi asked.

"Always."

"Do you have everything ready?" Jesi asked.

"We need to go by my house for the rest of the ingredients to finish the pouches. We've got to find them in two days, but I'm telling everyone we have until tomorrow night. Do you want to see if Chuck will join us for the search party tonight?"

Jesi nodded and wondered if it was right to pull Chuck further into the magical world.

~

Chuck drove up to Maggie's house on the outside of Coffee Bluff, not far from the CVS he was at earlier that day. There were already several cars in the driveway. The property must be at least two acres. The house looked like a bungalow with several extensions added. It had a second floor, and a garage built onto the left side of the house. He could see another structure sticking out from behind the garage. He thought it could be a storage shed, but it had too many windows for a storage building. The covered front porch had just enough room for matching rocking chairs. He decided it was Frankenstein's bungalow. It was even a shade of green.

He stepped out of his SUV and grabbed a backpack he packed with flashlights, bug spray, water, snacks, a first aid kit, and the knife made of iron Jesi told him to bring. He made his way to the front porch and noticed Maggie's friend, Emma, in one of the rocking chairs. Her dark hair was pulled into a ponytail and she rocked by pushing against the railing with her foot.

"Detective," she said and nodded her head in greeting. "Are you ready?"

"Emma," he said. "I am ready. Surprisingly enough, I

have participated in a search party before."

She stood up and smiled. "You've never participated in anything like this." She herded him through the front door and followed behind. "The detective is here," she yelled past him into the house.

The brightly decorated inside reminded him of the magic shop. To the left of the living room were stairs leading up to the second floor. He spied a dining table back to the right behind the living room and a door to the left of that he suspected led to the kitchen. There were several people crowded around the dining room table. He walked up to see a large map of the area laid out.

"These are the four areas that match the criteria of the spell best," Maggie said to the group. He counted 10 people around the table, and none looked up when he approached.

"The teams are decided upon," an older lady with a pointed nose and high cheekbones said. With her hair pulled into a tight bun at the base of her head, she looked severe and demanding. Everyone looked when she spoke. "We shall communicate via text. I suspect this young man is monitoring the magical traffic."

"Magical traffic?" Chuck asked before he could think better of it.

The lady looked up at him, her lips perfectly horizontal. "You must be Detective Massey, yes?" she said. "Alan's boy and subsequently, Jessica's new friend."

Chuck stared back without flinching. "Yes, ma'am," he said. She looked him up and down with a raised eyebrow.

"Jessica will explain," she said, then turned back to the group. "Do not deviate without communicating your location and plan. Be methodical and, most importantly, be careful."

She straightened up her back and pushed past the group toward the kitchen. Maggie appeared beside him and patted him on the shoulder.

"No worries, Chuckers," she said. "We're going to have fun tonight."

Her smile didn't reach her eyes as she motioned for him to follow her. She maneuvered through the kitchen and out the back door. Jesi was talking to Emma beside what he now saw was a greenhouse. When Jesi saw him, she smiled. It melted away any reservations he felt after his encounter with the old woman.

"I hear you met Sylvia," she said.

"Is that the lady with the bun and the pointed nose?" he asked.

"Yes," Jesi said. "She is the coven leader and my aunt. She is the oldest of Gigi's grandchildren."

"Wait," Chuck said, "you aren't Mrs. Watkin's grandchild?"

"No," she said, "I'm her great-grandchild."

"And this is Maggie's house," he said. "Why are we meeting here?"

"More room, and not so conspicuous as the shop, which is kinda close to downtown," Jesi said. "Tourist tend to stand around and stare. Good for business, but bad for keeping a low profile on the supernatural."

"Okay, you two," Maggie said. Emma and she walked

up to them, "we are group two, so let's pick a mode of transport and go."

"I vote sled dog," Emma said.

"I have an SUV with plenty of room," Chuck offered.

"Sled dog," Emma said. Maggie rolled her eyes.

"We can take my car," Jesi said. "It's big enough to fit all of us comfortably."

Emma turned to Maggie. "No sled dog?" she asked.

"Only if you want to be the dog," Maggie said, patting Emma on the head. Chuck looked at Jesi. She shrugged and led them to her SUV.

"What is magical traffic?" Chuck asked as they climbed in the car. "And where are we going?"

"You should have asked the second question before we climbed in the car," Emma said. Chuck could practically hear her smile, but he admitted she had a point.

"We are headed to area 2 on the map," Maggie said. "We are going to check out the wetlands preserve off of Highway 17 near Love's Seafood. It's one of the best spots in the area to cast the spell Roger is using."

"Magical traffic," Jesi said, "is a way of communicating with others using, well, magic. It's a convenient way to talk to someone in a magical telepathic way on these types of missions, but since he knows that we are on to him, he will most likely have an intercept spell or a disruption spell setup. Maggie and Sylvia agree that we shouldn't risk it."

"And it marks one of the few times that Maggie and Sylvia agree," Emma said.

"We always agree on the end goal," Maggie said. "We just don't always agree on how to get there."

"Can non-magical people use magical traffic?" Chuck asked.

"Yes," Maggie said. "It's the same with most other spells. Anyone can do it as long as you know how."

"I would just need to use the long way," Chuck said. "Right? With the long spell and herbs?"

"Correct," Emma said, deepening her voice. "Tell him what he's won."

"He's won an evening with three lovely ladies," Maggie said, mimicking Emma's tone, "searching for a lunatic."

"Are they always like this?" Chuck asked Jesi.

"Yep," Jesi said. "You'll learn what to ignore, don't worry."

Chapter 18

Jesi slumped onto the couch in Maggie's house. Built in the 1940s, Maggie inherited the house when her parents died in a car crash years ago. It was a little over two acres and a house bigger than they needed. Maggie said her parents hoped to have as many kids as possible. After years of trying, they finally gave birth to Maggie. By then, they were older and having one child was enough for them. But they always had nieces and nephews over to play and spend the night. It's one of the reason's Maggie was so close to everyone in the family and the coven. If anyone needed a place to stay, they could stay there. Maggie kept the same policy. Jesi had wonderful memories of this house, but sitting here now offered little comfort.

After they split up into four groups, they searched for hours looking for Roger's spot and found nothing. Even volunteers from the local wolf pack couldn't help. The scent was cold. Their group expanded the search beyond the wetland preserve going up and down the Ogeechee River. It proved a dead end.

When they got back to Maggie's, Chuck threw his hat into his car and drove off. Jesi wasn't sure when she'd see him again. What does it mean when he's mad or frustrated? Would he blame her? Would he pull away? Her feelings for him were growing fast, and when she watched him drive away, she remembered she did not in fact know that much about him.

She looked around when she heard Maggie bang around in the kitchen. It was too late, or else too early, and they were both too tired for Maggie to be cooking. Jesi heaved herself off the couch.

"Maggie, what are you doing?" she called.

Maggie rubbed shortening on a cookie sheet. She dropped it on the stove and went over to a large wooden bowl. "I'm making biscuits." She didn't look up.

"Why?" Jesi asked. "We are both exhausted."

"I need something to do," Maggie said. "I can't just sit here and do nothing. Those kids are going to die in two days. Roger could unleash Hell on earth, and we have no leads." She scooped baking powder and sprinkled salt into the flour, followed by a slow pour of butter milk.

"We both need rest. Even if it's just a few hours," Jesi said.

Maggie sighed. "We also need food."

"You have control over this, Maggie."

Maggie scooped more shortening from the container and plopped it into the buttermilk and worked the flour, milk, and shortening together.

"I have control over this bowl," Maggie said.

"You've started the spell pouches to counteract Roger," Jesi said. "And we have at least 15 people willing to help us fight. We are in control."

"We don't have those kids," Maggie said. Her shoulders shook.

Her hands stopped working the mixture and her hair fell in her face. Jesi pulled her into a hug. Maggie shook in Jesi's arms.

"I'm letting everyone down," she sobbed.

Cold, wet dough filled hands gripped Jesi's back, causing her to shiver, but she held tight to Maggie.

"No, you are not," Jesi said. "You are doing more than anyone else. You are not Gigi. No one expects you to be."

"But I feel like I should be," Maggie mumbled.

"The only one qualified to be Gigi was Gigi," Jesi said, using her lawyer voice. "And the only way we can do what she did is to work together."

Maggie's sobs slowed, and her breaths deepened. "It's so hard," Maggie said.

"It is so fucking hard," Jesi said. She squeezed Maggie tight.

"How are we going to pull this off?" Maggie asked.

"I don't know," Jesi said. "But between your knowledge and my gift, we will."

"What about Aunt Sylvia?" Maggie asked.

"I guess she can help." Jesi smiled into Maggie's hair when she heard Maggie giggle.

"Uh, I feel so stupid," Maggie said, pulling away from

Jesi's arms.

"But you aren't," Jesi said. "Let's get a nap. We only have, what, 40 hours to stop him, but we can't do it on zero sleep."

"Do you want any biscuits?" Maggie asked.

"Yes," Jesi said. "I want a batch of wet shirt biscuits."

Maggie laughed. She washed her hands and said, "I'll clean this up and get you a shirt."

~

After getting next to no sleep, Chuck stumbled into the precinct at his wit's end. He slumped into his desk. Thompson changed direction when Chuck shot him a look. Bastard basically refused to help with this case. He called it a lost cause and a few kids missing wasn't a big deal, especially when those kids were from the other side of the economic tracks. Thompson was a great cop when there was money to impress. It was no bother. He had a series of uniformed cops posted outside Roger's address and the bar he favored.

Chuck rubbed his hands over his face and logged into his computer. He couldn't stop thinking of Jesi's face. When he left, she had a permanent frown and heavy eyes. With a heavy heart and fueled with anger, he left Maggie's house. Last night was a huge bust. He didn't know what to expect from working with werewolves, but right now, he wasn't impressed. They didn't seem too impressed with him either.

"Massey."

His name hung in the air. No one looked up as Chuck drug himself into the captain's office.

"Massey," his captain said, "you've been on this kidnapping case for a week. What do you have for me?"

"I have a suspect," Massey said. He stood inside the door. Sitting in the captain's office wouldn't help him.

"And?"

"I can't find him," Chuck said. "I'm looking. And as you know, we put an APB out on him and Amber Alerts on the children."

"Well, look harder. Those cops from Macon will be here tomorrow to help. We'll work together to find these kids. Work with them. I know it's hard working with other departments, but this isn't a time to pull rank. Those kids are priority, not our egos. Go gather everything you have and get it ready to share. Now, get out of here."

Chuck left the office with a sigh and a frown. There was no use in telling the captain that having the cops from Macon coming tomorrow wouldn't be much help, not chasing magic. Roger was a ghost. He couldn't find him. He had a clean record. And someone willing to kidnap kids usually had a rap sheet.

He sat at his desk and typed Roger's name into the search one last time. Nothing would be different, but on the off chance it was, he checked anyway. They didn't even have a decent picture. His license picture was a few years old, before they put the license photos in the facial recognition database, and it was poor quality.

But he could find a good photo. Hayley. She had photos on social media.

Chuck opened his browser and pulled up his sister's Facebook page. She hadn't updated it in a few months, but she had a few photos of her with her new boyfriend. One without glasses and hats. Gotcha.

~

A continuous knock at the back door woke Jesi with a start. Her back complained as she sat up and looked around. Maggie's. She was still at Maggie's. She fell asleep on the couch. The sound continued. Maggie's head popped up from the floor. Her hair was sticking up everywhere. Ink splattered her right cheek. Papers and books covered the floor.

"What time is it?" Maggie asked. She reminded Jesi of a meerkat as she looked around the room.

Jesi checked her watch. "Uh, 9:30."

She stood up from the couch. Legs and back protested her movements. Maggie stood up and made her way to the kitchen and the noise. Jesi followed.

"What?" Maggie said as she unlocked the door.

Sylvia walked into the house. She looked Maggie up and down and nodded at Jesi.

"Time is precious, and we have little of it," Sylvia said.

"Well, thank you for stating the obvious," Maggie retorted.

Sylvia's lips turned downward as she sat on a stool at the kitchen island. "And the time we have can use less of your commentary."

"So, what brings you out to visit this early in the

morning?" Jesi asked.

"You usually call," Maggie added. She stood propped against the counter, arms crossed.

"Not all news is worthy of fanfare," Sylvia said, "And some news is best given in person."

"Oh, shit," Maggie said as she took a seat.

"Claudia Hester phoned me not two hours ago. I rushed to her side. Her son was taken in the night. He has a fledgling talent of temperature, but it's temperamental. Sometimes hot and sometimes cold and often nothing at all."

"And the scene?" Maggie asked.

"The same," Sylvia said. Her posture was somehow better than normal, and her face looked like a stone statue.

"Who is Claudia Hester?" Jesi looked between the two.

"She's a solitary witch in Brunswick," Sylvia said. "We repeatedly sent inquiries to achieve her membership, she always declined. I consider her a dear friend and ally."

"How old is her son?" Maggie asked.

"He's six." Sylvia smoothed out her dress. "The time is dire. Hours away from potential doom. We must gather our forces. Ten of our own will continue the search tonight, maybe more. And I have four promised from the wolves. If we can't find him tonight, we will be without the wolves tomorrow."

"Isn't it the first night of the full moon tonight?" Jesi asked.

"It is," Sylvia said. "And the four will be those born

with the affliction. They hold control from Morrighan herself. All will be well."

Jesi nodded her head at the explanation. The old books said that the Celtic Goddess, Morrighan, created werewolves. Of course, the story and name of the Goddess changed depending on culture and location. Those born a werewolf had complete control over themselves. They could shift at will and could maintain human form during a full moon. Those turned or bitten had no control over the shift and remained locked into the pull of the moon.

"So, we have ten witches, four wolves, and one detective?" Maggie asked. "That sounds just great. Hope we get there in time. Wouldn't want to have to battle a demi-demon on half power. Should I mention that it's really nine witches, four wolves, and two humans, one of which can cast spells if given the right tools?"

"Calm yourself, child." Sylvia's voice deepened, and she stood. The room began to close in on them. Jesi took a step back and clutched the counter. Maggie took a step forward.

"Do you think I would send you with anything less than the most experienced? The most skilled?" Sylvia appeared to look down on Maggie, despite Maggie being taller. "I, myself, will be by your side. No fight for our coven, on our soil, will be fought without its leader. So, it has always been, so shall it always be."

Jesi took a deep breath as the pressure in the room lightened. Maggie nodded, but didn't move. She stuck out her hand to Sylvia. They clasped forearms. It was a sign of mutual respect.

"Thank you," Maggie whispered.

Sylvia hugged her. Jesi didn't quite comprehend the realization that the two had at that moment. This may be the understanding and balance the two searched for this past year. Or it may fall apart once they save the children. Either way, Jesi knew she could breathe easier now that those two met eye to eye.

"Meet here two hours 'til moonrise. I will relay the message myself. Keep the witch line open. Tell no one of the last missing child." Sylvia left with one word as she walked out the door. "Tonight."

Jesi walked Sylvia to her car and watched her drive out of sight. She turned and surveyed the house. The sage smell fell heavily in the air. Extra lavender hung on each corner of the roof. Maggie made her way to the greenhouse. Jesi watched Maggie move back and forth through the windows as she gathered more stuff together. Jesi joined her.

"Do you think she'll wear a dress for battle?" Jesi asked.

Maggie stopped and looked at Jesi with a frown. "That is a good question. She didn't wear a dress yesterday, but it's a toss-up. I assume she'll wear the heels as a weapon though. Nothing is worse than getting stabbed with a shoe."

"That's your nothing worse?" Jesi raised an eyebrow.

"Today it is."

Chapter 19

Maggie slammed her book shut. "We have less than three hours until moonrise and we have no clue where that little shit is," she said.

"I know," Jesi sighed. She stretched out her hands. She was no closer to cracking the rune on Hayley. "It looks like we are zero for two. Do we have any other options?" Jesi asked.

"I have another list of places for the spell he's most likely to cast," Maggie said. "I've narrowed it to ten locations."

"That's better than a million." Jesi rubbed her face.

"Still too many to search in this amount of time. Some are far off." Maggie put her head in her hands.

A loud bang, bang, bang came from the front door. Jesi and Maggie looked at each other. Maggie looked at her watch.

"Someone is really early or really mad," Jesi said.

She made her way to the front door. The loud

knocking continued until she opened it. Chuck stood in front of her. His eyes were wide, and he panted.

"Jesi," he said. He grabbed her by her arms, which crumpled the papers he held in one hand. "We got him."

"What?" Jesi asked.

"WE have him." Chuck hugged Jesi and pushed her into the house. He shoved the papers into her hands. "His name isn't Roger Hall. It's Roger Gaines. He was born and raised in North Carolina. His mother died when he was young, and his father raised him. He works for a shell company. They own three properties in the area. All three are in secluded areas. He's got to be at one of those locations. I traced the shell company to a holding company in North Carolina called Cernunnos, Inc. They are supposedly a consulting company for creating extreme camping expeditions."

"That sounds dumb," Maggie said as she joined them. "But Cernunnos sounds familiar."

"Like the Celtic God, Cernunnos," said Jesi.

"The God of Beasts and Wild Places," Maggie said, "the horned one. Some see him as the God of Hunters." Jesi's eyes grew wide and looked toward Chuck. He scrunched his brows together.

"What's with the looks?" Chuck asked. "Why is the God of Hunters important?"

"Long ago," Maggie started, "like thousands of years ago, the supernatural community, the witches, the wolves, various Fae, changelings, shifters, minor deities, and half-demons had a mutual relationship with the hunters. The hunters would protect the humans from the supernatural that actively attacked the humans and also protect the supernatural from the humans that came after us. They were the justice system that kept those that wished to expose us to the world either through terror or other reasons from being known to the average person. They kept the balance between the supernatural and the humans. About a hundred years ago, their power went to their head, and began to strike down all supernatural beings. Peaceful or not, they struck them down. Local communities started policing ourselves, and protecting each other. I've heard rumors of hunting groups who keep to the old ways, but we haven't sought them out. The risk is too dangerous."

"If Roger is working for a hunter group and kidnapping supernatural children, it's a good bet they are not here for hugs and donuts," Jesi said.

"But we have three locations to check out?" Maggie asked.

"Yeah, it's taken me all day to track down any locations in the area associated with his employer and gather search warrants for each location," Chuck said. "Technically, the police are going to issue the warrants tomorrow when the cops from Macon get here."

"You have search warrants?" Maggie asked. "Damn boy. And it's better than the 10 maybes we had before, but it's getting late. I'm going to compare your locations with my own. We'll split up into groups once everyone gets here." Maggie took the papers from Jesi and walked further into the house.

"I'm glad you came back," Jesi said. After he left last

night, she wasn't sure if he'd want to work with them again.

"I always planned on coming back," Chuck said. "I felt like I let you down. I was pretty useless during the search party." He smiled down at her.

Jesi returned the smile. She could feel the tension in her shoulders dissipate, and she moved in and wrapped her arms around him.

"I think we all felt that way." Jesi breathed him in and tightened her grip. "How much trouble will you be in for not waiting until tomorrow morning?"

"Enough," Chuck said, "but I should be fine as long as we find the children."

"I don't know what you two are doing, but save it for tomorrow," Maggie called from the back of the house.

Jesi bounced on the balls of her feet while she held on to Chuck. They were going to do this. They could stop him. She felt a buzz of hope through her and she knew Chuck felt it too. Jesi let go and slid out of his arms. His blue eyes smiled at her. She grabbed his hand and pulled him toward the back of the house. Once in the kitchen, Emma walked through the back door with her brother and two other wolves whose names she didn't remember.

"What's wrong?" Maggie asked.

"We have a slight problem," Emma said, crossing her arms over her chest.

"Define slight," Chuck asked.

"Since when does the human get to ask questions?" Emma asked.

"Since he narrowed down the location of Roger, the bad guy, to three places instead of ten," Maggie said.

"Fair enough," Emma said. "One of our cubs bit a teacher."

"And they don't want to come with you to the pack?" Maggie asked.

"No. We can't find her," Emma said. She looked like she ate a sour grape, and her eyes had a slight glow.

"When was she bitten?" Maggie asked.

"Two days ago. And we are not sure exactly who she is."

"Shit. And too late for the antidote," Maggie said. Her fingers drummed on the island.

"You don't know the kid's teacher?" Chuck asked.

"It was a substitute," Spencer, Emma's brother, said. "The name is Ms. Maddy. We've been to every house with a Maddy in three counties. This could end in death across the low country."

"Or an outbreak we won't be able to contain," one man behind Emma said.

"Do you have a description?" Chuck asked.

"Yeah. You think you can help us find her?" Emma asked.

"I can call in a missing person's report. And contact the school for details on Ms. Maddy," Chuck said.

Jesi could feel him stand up a little straighter behind her.

"It's Sunday. There is no one to call," one of the wolfs said.

"I have my ways. Description?" Chuck asked. He

pulled out his small pad and pen.

"She's tall, with blonde hair, and blue eyes," Emma said.

"That's all you have?" Chuck raised an eyebrow.

"That's all a six-year-old would give me," Emma said.

"Next time, call me. I'll use my gift," Jesi said. "Where was she bitten?"

"On the hand or wrist," Emma said.

"Blonde hair, blue eyes, hand, Maddy," Jesi said. Something about that combination jogged her memory. She moved to the kitchen island with her papers, picked up her pen, and started writing out runes again.

"Wynn, os, lagu, feoh," she said out loud as she wrote the runes over one another. She held up the finished rune mark.

"Wolf," she said.

"That's the tattoo," Maggie said.

"Not Maddy, Massey. Massey. Ms. Massey. She's a substitute teacher," Chuck said, his mouth wide open. "She's a werewolf?"

Jesi swallowed hard and nodded. She put down the paper and wrapped her arms around him. Four days ago, magic was a fairy tale, and now he swam in it. Chuck clutched Jesi, buried his face in the crook of her neck. She could hear him breathe heavily as he shook his head.

~

Jesi rubbed Chuck's back. He could hardly breathe. His sister was not only in the hands of a madman, but was also a werewolf. What could he possibly do to help her now? He tried to calm his breathing. He focused on Jesi rubbing his back. Up and down. In and out. Up and down. In and out.

He half listened to the surrounding conversation. Maggie explained that Hayley Massey was his sister and Alan's daughter. Emma mentioned being able to use Chuck's scent to track her better. Or maybe he had access to some of her stuff.

Chuck clung to Jesi. In and out. He took in Jesi's scent. Lavender and sage from being in the shop and Maggie's house all day. The soft words she spoke helped him concentrate. It would be okay. Hayley would still be Hayley. Emma was normal. Hayley would have a support system. The only thing he had to do now was find her.

Chuck rested his forehead against Jesi's and looked into her eyes. "Thank you," he whispered. He composed himself and looked toward the wolves, the werewolves. "I'll do whatever you need to help," he said.

"Great," Emma said. "Do you have access to anything that might have her scent on it? And we will need it quickly."

"Yeah. My dad still has her jumpsuit at his shop," Chuck said.

"Can you call and let him know that someone will pick it up soon?" Emma asked. She turned to one of the guys behind her and said, "Spence, please run by there and pick it up?"

Chuck nodded as the other guy rushed out the door. Chuck hesitated as he pulled out his phone. He texted his dad instead of calling. 'I'll explain later,' was the last line. How would he tell his father that Hayley was now a werewolf? Sure, wolves worked in the shop, but it's different when your daughter is one herself. He felt a warm hand on his arm.

"It'll be alright," Jesi said.

Thirty minutes later, Spencer was back with Hayley's jumpsuit. It had Lil' M monogrammed on the upper right side. Chuck could only stare at it as the four wolves smelled the garment. Members of the coven began to arrive. Chuck didn't pay much attention to the first few as they came into the kitchen.

Until one commanded his attention and everyone else's in the room. It was Sylvia. He paid close attention to her now. She was older than the others, with silver-streaked hair tight in a bun. She glided across the room in tailored jeans and a leather jacket. Her belt reminded Chuck of Batman's utility belt, only with small leather bags attached as compartments. He heard a loud wolf whistle sound off behind him.

"Damn, Sylvia," Emma said. "How you doin'?"

"Must you be uncouth?" Sylvia asked. She stood there with her hands clasped in front, her back straight. Chuck looked around. Everyone watched her and waited, except Emma. She stretched and raised an eyebrow when he made eye contact with her.

"Aunt Sylvia," Maggie said. "Chuck found some information regarding Roger. He works for a company called Cernunnos."

"No. Not hunters," Sylvia said. "This is a dark day

indeed. When once the hunters kept peace among the supernatural, now they hunt us down like dogs."

"What do you think he is looking for?" Jesi asked.

Sylvia shook her head. "I don't know. Yet, there is a reason I never permitted him to join the coven."

"I thought he didn't want to join," said Maggie.

"No, he asked," Sylvia said. "I told him no. A sister says his aura is damaged. His soul is not steady. He was a risk we could not take."

Chuck looked around the room. Everyone was quiet. It was a lot to take in. So many things in the balance and so much to lose if they failed.

"Tonight," Sylvia said in a voice that brought everyone's attention to the front, "we hunt. Evil calls upon the dark forces. Children are in the line of fire and innocence is at stake. Evil expects defensive action. Tonight, we bring offense. The Moonlight Oak Coven and the Old Moss Pack are not reactive. Tonight, we snuff the flame that takes our people."

Chuck felt chills down his spine when she spoke. He nodded along with her words and saw the others follow suit. Jesi grabbed his hand and squeezed it hard.

"Okay, here is the plan," Maggie started. She laid out a map on the island beside the bags of spell materials, and Jesi handed out sheets to all the witches. "We will split into three groups. We have it narrowed down between three locations. As soon as the right location is found and you have eyes on the kids and Hayley, call the other groups so they can assist as fast as possible. Do nothing until the other groups arrive."

"So, what exactly do we know about this spell he's trying to perform?" one of the witches asked.

"It's a summoning spell for a minor demon," Maggie said.

"How minor?" Spencer asked.

"Based on the ingredients he's bought and the tattoo design, it's most likely a seeker demon," Maggie told the group. "He is searching for something and needs demonic help."

"And what is he looking for?" Jesi asked.

"We don't know," Sylvia said.

"How dangerous are these minor demons?" Chuck asked.

"They are extremely dangerous, both to the caster and to everyone else," Sylvia said with a frown. "They are more like tricksters. They will find what you want, but will break off from the caster as soon as possible, and are some of the harder ones to pull back into the Underworld."

"Have you done anything like this before?" Chuck asked. He wasn't sure who he was asking. Everyone, he supposed.

"Gigi had," Sylvia said. "She was a lot stronger than the rest of us. We might need more than one of us saying the spell at the same time."

"If this demon gets inside of Hayley?" Chuck asked. It was his worst fear. A stone dropped in his stomach when he asked the question.

"It won't. The demon will consider her too corrupted to possess, because she's a werewolf," Maggie said. "It will either go for one of the kids or for Roger. Roger would be the best bet. Stronger, older."

"What will Roger do when he realizes that Hayley can't be used?" another witch asked.

"He has a few options," Maggie said. "Though, he shouldn't cast the spell tonight. It's stronger if cast on the full moon. Hayley will change tonight. Once Roger realizes this, he will either mark himself for the spell, use one of the children, or coerce another person and mark them."

"And this antidote for werewolves," Chuck said. "you're sure it's too late?"

"Yeah. It only works 48 hours after infection or until the full moon rises, whichever comes first," Jesi said. "She was bitten Friday morning. The tattoo was different Sunday morning. I think it changed right at the 48 hour mark." She reached over and squeezed his shoulder. He nodded at her.

"I'm going to kill Roger," he said.

"Only after we get information out of him," Maggie said to the group. "You got that, people? We want this bastard alive."

"Maggie, why are you ruining our fun?" Emma asked. Chuck saw Jesi roll her eyes and shake her head.

"Maggie speaks with wisdom beyond her years," Sylvia said. "This could be the beginning of something much worse. Knowledge is the root of all power."

The group moved around and gathered supplies. Chuck stayed close to Jesi.

"So, Sylvia is your and Maggie's aunt?" he asked. "You said your mom isn't interested in participating.

What about Maggie's parents?"

"Maggie's parents died a few years ago," Jesi said. "Sylvia is our aunt. She is the oldest of her siblings."

"How does your mom feel about you being so involved?" He asked.

"I haven't told her." Jesi smiled. "She's still mad I received a power, so we don't discuss coven business."

Chapter 20

Chuck handed out the addresses owned by Cernunnos, Inc. After the heated discussion regarding how to divide the groups, they split up. They had exactly one day to find Roger and stop his spell. Maggie insisted the spell was the most powerful if performed during the full moon.

Apparently, the moon, while only technically full for one night, still affected were-creatures for three nights total. The night before the full moon, the night of the full moon, and the night after. Chuck had her explain this several times. He still couldn't quite wrap his head around it. He was even more confused when she tried to explain why the wolves helping them today could control their change. He conceded that all he really needed to know was that his sister would now become a wolf three nights a month and would not be able to control when she shifted. And he needed to stop Roger before she died. He wasn't convinced Roger wouldn't kill her once she turned into a werewolf.

Chuck climbed into his SUV with Jesi, Maggie, and Emma. Everyone agreed to call the other groups and wait as soon as they found Roger's hideout. Chuck insisted everyone wait for the other groups before engaging. He didn't become a detective because of his good looks. Experience and knowledge were his strong suits. And trusting his co-workers helped.

Chuck parked the SUV along the road. The address was outside the city limits, and to maintain the element of surprise, they stayed out of the driveway. Maggie looked at the group as they gathered around.

"Okay," she said, "Emma goes first. We follow. Everyone has a pouch of the counter spell, just in case. Remember, we need to light it on fire and say the spell. Light it and drop it if you have to, but say the spell."

Maggie and Jesi attached the pouches to their belts like Sylvia. Chuck and Emma put theirs in their pockets.

"There is no way this guy is doing the spell tonight," Emma said. "He'll need the extra boost from tomorrow's moon."

Emma's eyes shined bright in the darkness. They made Chuck shift on his feet and move slightly in front of Jesi. Emma smiled at him and shook her head.

"Remember," Chuck said. "We call for backup if this is the place. No need to run in with our guns blazing."

They all nodded. Emma looked around, sniffed the air, and made her way through the woods. Maggie walked in her footsteps, followed by Jesi and Chuck doing the same. Emma looked like she was right at home stalking through the woods. Maggie didn't seem to have much trouble either. Jesi, on the other hand, moved slower and tripped her way along. Chuck caught her each time she shifted backwards. She didn't look like someone who would lose their balance. Chuck thought about the way she pushed through a room. She took a hard step. Walking lightly wasn't her thing.

~

Jesi breathed a sigh of relief when they came to the edge of the woods that looked out onto a rundown farmhouse with a barn in the background. The house was dark, but the barn's lights burned brightly.

Emma turned and whispered to the group, "We just crossed some sort of barrier. I can smell people, where I couldn't five feet back. I'm going to look around. Stay here."

She skirted along the edge of the woods and made her way across the lawn to the house and around the back. Chuck's hand was at Jesi's back. It kept her steady while crouched down among the brush.

"Here she comes," Maggie whispered.

Jesi didn't see Emma for another 30 seconds. Could Maggie sense her? She often wondered how close Emma and Maggie really were, even after gleaning Maggie on an almost daily basis.

"No one is in the house," Emma said. "The only scent I smelled is a day old. There are several scents coming from the barn, including Hayley's."

Jesi felt Chuck move and stop. He breathed louder.

She grabbed his hand and squeezed, pulling him up behind her. They followed Emma around the back of the house. The closer they got to the barn, the more dread Jesi felt. They all stopped short at the same time.

"Something's not right," Jesi said.

"I smell evil here." Emma stared at the barn, her eyes wide.

"I'm texting the others," Maggie said, pulling out her phone. "We should go back to the front of the house and wait."

"What is that?" Chuck asked, pointing toward the barn.

Jesi looked around the barn until she spotted it. It bounced up and down through the weeds towards them. It was a pale blue color with sharp tipped ears and matching teeth with hair sticking straight up. Then she saw more. Bright blue ones, who barely flew above the grass, and looked like they were made of sharp edges. There were green ones with horns and long hair, and red ones with large mouths.

"Bogeys," Maggie said. Jesi barely heard her through her sharp intake of breath. "And red ragers and foul Fae."

She reached in her pocket for the knife she brought. An iron knife she never used, because she never needed it. Maggie pulled what looked like a short sword from God knows where, and Emma did the same.

"What's a bogey and a rager?" Chuck asked.

"Bad faeries. Like the ones at Sandy's house," Jesi said, "only evil."

"They are evil Fae, the kind that whisper in your ear,

encouraging your bad thoughts," Maggie said. "I've never heard of them fighting in the open like this. He must have promised them something extraordinary. Did you bring a weapon of iron?"

"Yeah," Chuck said, pulling his own knife from his side.

"It's worse," Emma said. She pointed past the small army of Fae that moved toward them. "He's starting the ritual tonight."

Just inside the entrance of the barn, they could see a fire with two children on either side. Roger stood on one end and Hayley sat at the other, like they were all seated at a table, only the fire was the table. Roger's hands were over his head with his face to the sky.

"We can't wait," Chuck said. "Let's make a path for Maggie and Jesi." Chuck started forward beside Emma into battle with the tiny Fae.

The idea that dangerous bogeys and red ragers fought for Roger was mind boggling. How did you get any faery to fight on your side? What did he promise? What could he give them? If he didn't deliver, he would pay dearly. He needed to pay dearly, and she wasn't above letting the Fae take a chunk of his hide.

Jesi swiped at the bogeys coming toward her. She used her elbows and knife and even stomped on a few. She was behind Maggie and pushed her forward. The little Fae moved in on them all, and it looked like Maggie was their main target. One was hanging off of her counter spell pouch, but Jesi couldn't reach it and Maggie was busy holding off the ones coming at her front.

It started to get harder to see. The sun began to set, and they weren't close enough to the fire to benefit from its light. That's when she heard it.

~

Chuck's head popped up from the battle.

"I can't," Hayley said. "I can't. I can't hold on. I can't stop."

Roger's chant paused. Chuck saw his sister sway and shake her head. Her hands grabbed her hair.

"What are you doing?" Roger asked.

"I can't stop," Hayley said even louder. Her breathing became ragged and the bogey Chuck was fighting bit his ear.

"Oww," he yelled. It pulled his attention away from his sister. He pulled bitey off his ear and stabbed another coming up on the other side. He wanted a sword like Maggie and Emma.

"Nothing should be happening yet," he heard Roger say. "It's too soon. Stop moving."

A loud growl rumbled through the area. The Fae stopped the fight at the sound, only to start back in the next second.

"Don't touch me," Hayley said. Her voice sounded deeper than normal, but held the grit and anger that Chuck knew. That was his sister, full of piss and vinegar.

"What is happening to you?" Roger asked.

Chuck swung his knife and kicked at another creature. They all reminded him of tiny devils, of all colors. They moved closer to the fire. He heard his sister scream as he fought these things off. He could only look up at sporadic intervals. His sister was changing, and fast.

He tried to run for her, but the creatures pulled him down. He swiped and stabbed them and stood back up. Chuck looked toward the barn in time to see his sister howl behind the fire. Roger reached for her, but the wolf snapped at him. Roger shrank away in time for Hayley to jump over him and the fire. Emma took off after Hayley and left Jesi, Maggie, and him to fight the Fae. Emma's speed surprised Chuck, but he didn't have time to dwell on that because the number of tiny creatures appeared to grow. Chuck saw Roger raise up his knife.

Chapter 21

Jesi watched Roger raise his knife.

"This will not stop me. We must finish this," Roger bellowed.

"NO!" Chuck yelled.

Roger didn't turn. He cut his own arm. Blood dripped down. Jesi almost heard the words Roger chanted. She feared for the children. She saw them squirm around the fire and heard them through the gags. The Fae took advantage of her distraction and pulled her to the ground.

As she fell, Maggie and Chuck fell too, but Maggie stopped fighting. The Fae let go of all of them and they jumped up and down in victory. Jesi took advantage of the moment and rushed to Maggie. She was out cold, but breathing. Her head hit a rock. The pouch on Maggie's side was shredded, so was Jesi's. Jesi looked around and saw Chuck stand up; then she rushed toward Roger with nothing but herself and her knife covered in Fae blood.

Black tendrils climbed up Roger's leg. He kept chanting as it moved up his body, yet he was still ready for her and blocked her. The blood flowed from his newly cut wound, and dark coils slid into the gash, yet he managed to kick Jesi back.

He stayed close to the fire and the children. She smiled at him and knew in that moment that he was playing defense. She may not have the pouch, but she had the words, and she pulled them out of her pocket.

She began speaking the counter spell. His spell wavered as wind whipped around her head. She felt the pull of magic from her gut. It rushed through her veins and out her fingertips. She walked closer to the fire as she spoke. She finished the spell, but she needed to say it two more times. She faltered.

Jesi looked at the faces of the kids and chanted louder. Her own power pushed out of her and around the fire, but she wasn't strong enough. She shook the more she spoke. Her center of balance failed, and she fell to her knees, but she continued.

She saw a bright flash in the fire and felt a hand grasp her own. Chuck was there. His own pouch, the extra, thrown into the flame. She felt her magic connect and grow from the link with him. She repeated the spell, louder than before. From the fire, the ingredients flickered over the hot embers. The magic burned throughout her.

"So, mote it be," she said.

With her free hand, she pushed out the power toward Roger, which pushed him down breathlessly as his own spell died. Jesi let go of Chuck and walked toward Roger. A little darkness that tried to reach him retreated into the earth, into the fire that burned down to hot coals. Jesi grabbed his throat.

"Why are you here?" His life and memories rushed into her system. She tightened her grip.

"I'll never tell you," he said.

"You already have." Jesi let him go.

"More will come," he spat at her. "Your kind will cease to be."

"Roger Gaines? You have the right to remain silent," Chuck began as he rolled Roger onto his stomach and cuffed him. The bogeys and ragers and Fae from earlier jumped onto Roger's back. Chuck stepped back and looked at Jesi open-mouthed. The Fae tore chunks of hair out of Roger's head and slashed at his arms and legs with their nails. As quickly as they started, they stopped and vanished into the night.

"What happened?" Chuck asked as he felt Roger's pulse. "He's out cold now."

"He's been marked," Maggie said. "He must have promised something he can no longer deliver. They will come back for him or curse him or something."

"Maggie, you're awake!" Jesi said and hugged her.

"Ouch," Maggie said, shaking Jesi off. "I'm still in a lot of pain. I have a killer headache. And no idea what exactly happened."

"Jesi was a badass, that's what," Emma said coming out of the darkness with a gray wolf chasing its tail beside her.

"Hayley?" Chuck said, moving toward the wolf.

"Let's back up there," Emma said. "She's not quite herself yet. It will take a couple of moons for her wolf and her human side to communicate."

"The kids," Jesi said and rushed to free them. Jesi and Chuck untied the children and held them tight. Jesi shuttered slightly as the memories flooded her mind, but she held tight to two of the children as they shook and buried their faces in her embrace. Chuck held the others and rocked them slightly.

"And the Calvary is here," Emma said. The three other groups were running toward them from the old house.

"Quick," Maggie said. She fished around in Jesi's pockets. Jesi didn't let go of the children, despite the intrusion. Maggie pulled out the power stripping potion.

"How did you..." Jesi began.

"No time," Maggie said. She moved to Roger's side and pulled his unconscious body up into a sitting position and yanked his head back. Emma joined her and held his mouth open.

"I don't know what your power is," Maggie said as she poured the potion down his throat, "but you won't use it ever again."

Jesi stared in disbelief. All the research she'd done on that potion indicated that using it against the wishes of the surrounding supernatural community leaders was akin to the actions of a traitor. What would happen to Maggie if they found out?

"What happened to you waiting?" Sylvia asked.

Everyone turned to face her.

"He already started the spell," Jesi said. "We had to move fast."

"You're glowing," Sylvia said, "just like your Gigi. And the detective, too."

"What?" Jesi looked down. Her brown skin glowed bright in the moonlight. She looked at Chuck. He glowed as well. She didn't notice it before.

"It happens when you call on the powers around you or call on a specific power," Sylvia nodded at Chuck.

"Well, Chuckers, you're in and we'll kill you if you hurt her, blah blah blah, I need some sleep," Maggie said and walked away. Her phone rang as she walked. "Hey Vera," she said. She continued toward the house and Jesi could no longer hear her conversation.

Chuck smiled at Jesi. "I'm going to call this in," he said. "Y'all should clear out."

"You're going to have a hell of a time explaining this," Jesi said.

"I'm more worried about explaining the glow," he said.

Chapter 22

Jesi looked around Maggie's living room. She had her legs on Chuck's lap while Maggie and Emma sat on the other chairs. Jesi took a deep breath and explained, for what she hoped would be the last time, what she saw when she touched Roger.

"It took me a few days to sort out exactly what I saw when I grabbed Roger," Jesi began. "He was half possessed by the demon at that point. I saw part of Roger's life and part of the demon's. They blended and mushed together. But, with the help of Chuck, I think I've pieced together Roger's life. I know what he was after and why." Chuck squeezed her hand and she continued.

"He didn't have a great childhood. His mother was a witch. His father was human. His father found out about his mom and was extremely angry that she kept it from him. His mom died shortly after. Roger was told all his life that she died because of her magic and that it would kill him too. Chuck thinks the father killed her. Roger grew up being punished for being a witch. He wanted to get rid of his magic and with it, everyone else's magic. He found a hunter's group with a similar goal. There, the group fueled his obsession. They are looking for a way to end all paranormal creatures and magic."

"How do they plan to do that?" Emma asked.

"They are looking for something or someone called the Holder of Knowledge or the Book of Knowledge. They sent Roger because his witch power gave him the ability to read and understand any text in any language. He couldn't write in the languages though, which I find interesting. He was summoning a demon that could find it. A demon good at finding things. The demon of hidden secrets."

"Well, I guess we need to prepare for more of these hunters," Emma said. "And look into this Book of Knowledge."

"Yesterday, Aunt Sylvia told me the book is a legend," Maggie said. "She thinks we shouldn't bother."

"Sounds like we're going to look anyway," Emma said. She smiled at Maggie. "Hey, why did the bad faeries stop fighting when Maggie went down? And what did Roger promise them?"

"Roger told them that Maggie was the real threat and that the rest of us couldn't stop him," Jesi said. "And he promised them the throne of the Fae world, which means free rein with no consequences. And all of Savannah."

"Dumb," Maggie replied. "And of course, we are going after that book." Maggie and Emma high-fived.

"How's your sister, Chuckers?"

"She's learning and doing better," Chuck said and rolled his eyes at Maggie's nickname for him. "She doesn't feel like she's walking around in a fog anymore and hopes to work at the shop again soon. But I'm still worried about her. My mom says she wakes up screaming at night."

"I'll go visit her." Maggie frowned. "It may be a side effect of being under that spell for so long. I might have something that can help her."

"She's done well accepting that she's a werewolf," Emma said. "I think she already had an idea that they existed. But there is still a transition period for her. How are the kids?"

"The kids are all home safe," Jesi said. "Surprisingly, Roger didn't physically harm them too much. He pricked their fingers for the spell. Most of the damage he did was psychological, which in my opinion, is worse. Sylvia promised to find them all counseling. Maggie is working on a potion to help them sleep for the short term. All the families are willing to testify against Roger. They are actually demanding to testify. They know a decent lawyer."

"Speaking of lawyers and lawsuits," Maggie said. "Chuckers, do you want to show her?"

Jesi watched Chuck and Maggie smile at each other, then Chuck moved Jesi's legs off of his lap. He stood and pulled Jesi up to follow him into the dining room with the other two ladies behind them.

"I, well, we would like to show you a picture," Chuck

said.

Jesi looked down at the table, at a single drawing. It was of the magic shop. It had a second door on the front with a sign over it that read, "Moonlight Oak Law Firm, LLC."

"What is this?" Jesi asked. She looked at the three people in front of her, who all smiled like Cheshire cats.

"We want to know what you think of quitting my shop and moving upstairs to open up your own law firm," Maggie said.

"You can help the little people this time," Chuck said.

"And if you decide you like the name we chose, the local supernatural community will know you are a safe space for them to come with their legal needs," Maggie said. "With that said, you don't have to keep that name."

"So, I would go from being a corporate attorney to opening a... general practice firm?" Jesi asked. She picked up the picture. "You two worked together on this?"

"Yes," Chuck said.

"And Emma. She knows a good contractor we can call," Maggie added.

"I called Maggie two days ago to ask what she thought of the idea," Chuck said. "Apparently she'd been thinking about something similar for a while."

"It's still a rough idea," Maggie said. "And we didn't kill each other. Though, I think Chuckers thought about it every time I said his name."

"You never call me by my name," Chuck said through gritted teeth.

Jesi smiled at the two of them as they bickered.

"I love this," Jesi said. "And I love the name." She pulled them away from the glaring contest and into an enormous hug. "Thank you. So, so much." Jesi felt tears fall down her face. She pulled back and wiped her eyes.

"What's wrong, Jesi?" Chuck placed his hand on her cheek and rubbed away the tears with his thumb.

"Nothing," Jesi said. She smiled and leaned into his hand. "This is all so perfect. I don't deserve it."

Chuck pulled Jesi into a hug. She breathed in his scent and sunk into his embrace. Everything was changing for her once again, but it wasn't overwhelming this time.

"Of course, you do," Maggie said. "We'll leave you two alone now."

Maggie and Emma left out the back door. Jesi leaned back to look up into Chuck's blue eyes.

"So, are you still planning on taking me on a date?" she asked.

He leaned in and gave her a quick kiss.

"We can go on a date whenever you like," he said. "We can also go back to my place instead."

Jesi captured his mouth with her own. She sucked at his bottom lip just long enough for him to open for her. She ended the kiss and said, "Let's go to your place first."

Acknowledgements

I want to thank my husband for supporting me throughout this journey. He has encouraged me from day one.

I also want to thank my son for giving sage advice, such as, a cop without a beard looks like a robot. Everyone should have a six-year-old on hand.

I send thanks and love to my mom and my sister for giving honest feedback on all of my questions of varying strangeness. They have both supported my writing and encouraged others to read my words. I would be lost without them.

My beta readers and sensitivity reader are the greatest and brought out the best of this story. Thank you from the bottom of my heart.

Lastly, I want to thank the Indie Babe Support Group Discord that have helped with everything from blurb advice to easing the tension with laughs.

About the Author

Lucille Yates enjoys writing the stories that are constantly playing like a movie in her head. She is excited that others will now enjoy them as much as she does.

When she is not writing, she is reading, playing with her six-year-old son, watching videos, or playing games. She lives outside of Savannah, GA with her husband, son, and four cats.

Did you enjoy this book? Please review and visit Lucille's website for updates, sign up for her newsletter, and learn how to find her across social media.

www.lucilleyateswrites.com

The Wolf's Return - A Bite of Magic Book 2
coming soon.